BOOTS & CHAPS

UGLY STICK SALOON BOOK #1

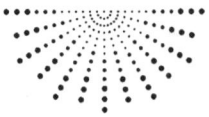

MYLA JACKSON

ELLE JAMES

TWISTED PAGE INC

BOOTS & CHAPS

UGLY STICK SALOON BOOK #1

New York Times & USA Today
Bestselling Author
ELLE JAMES

writing as

MYLA JACKSON

Previously released by Samhain Publishing.

EBOOK ISBN: 978-1-62695-090-0

PRINT ISBN: 978-1-62695-091-7

DEDICATION

This book is dedicated to those readers who love a sexy hero (or heroine) in boots and chaps!

ABOUT THIS BOOK

Passions burn between a Kiowa cowboy and a red-hot former stripper

It's Jackson Gray Wolf's thirtieth birthday, and he has little to show for it. No woman, no kids and no prospects for dates. Sure, the Kiowa cowboy has a ranch and two younger brothers, but he's in a rut where women are concerned, until the pretty little owner of the Ugly Stick Saloon captures his attention. A hot encounter in the saloon storeroom ends before he can get her out of studded red cowboy boots.

Audrey Anderson is trying to shake her former occupation as a stripper and project her new role as the savvy business owner of the Ugly Stick Saloon. Now instead of taking off her own clothes, she manages a bevy of strippers. When one of her strippers calls in sick, she's forced to slip on a mask and into her role as the kinky Kiki Cox for the Gray Wolf twins surprise party for their older brother. Not that she minds, not after a sizzling near miss with Jackson in her own storeroom.

His mind on the red boots and tight tush of a certain saloon owner, Jackson doesn't want the birthday party his twin brothers are throwing. But his promise to ignore the stripper goes awry when she shows him just how willing she is to please him and his brothers.

Audrey gives them her all, but fears the one she wants might be more interested in the sexy stripper Kiki than the tamer saloon owner, Audrey.

This is a reprint of Boots and Chaps from Samhain Publishing

Warning: This story contains hot Kiowa cowboy brothers and a former stripper in a heart-stoppingly HOT *menage a trois*!

AUTHOR'S NOTE

Enjoy other Ugly Stick Saloon books by Myla
Jackson

Visit Mylajackson.com for more information
Or visit her alter ego Elle James at ellejames.com
Join Elle James and Myla Jackson's Newsletter at
http://ellejames.com/ElleContact.htm

CHAPTER ONE

*J*ackson Gray Wolf had just about had enough of the loud music, shouts from drunken cowboys and the smell of alcohol that permeated the air at the Ugly Stick Saloon. If not for the company of the owner-bartender, Audrey Anderson, he'd have left hours ago and returned to collect his twin brothers, Mark and Luke, at last call.

Mark whirled by on the dance floor to a lively two-step, a red-haired cowgirl tucked tightly against his body.

"About ready to head home?" Jackson called out as his brother turned and guided his partner toward the other end of the floor.

"Nope." Mark twirled the girl and hollered, "Hell yeah!" to the song the band was playing.

Luke swung by with a pretty brunette. "Maybe an hour?" He grinned broadly. "Why aren't you dancin'?"

Jackson shrugged. "Not in the mood." Truth was, he hadn't been *in the mood* for the past six months. With his thirtieth birthday fast approaching, he'd fallen into a funk the size of Texas and couldn't figure out why. The girls there tonight were just that…girls. Young girls, silly girls, girls who giggled at nearly every word he said. Where were the more mature women?

"What's got you down, Jackson?" Audrey plunked a cup of coffee in front of him and leaned over the counter, her brow wrinkled into a frown. "You haven't been yourself lately."

"Who said there's somethin' wrong?" He curled his fingers around the mug, letting the heat warm him.

"You used to be out there dancing with the twins like it was some kind of race."

"I'm gettin' too old for that nonsense."

She straightened, her brows rising into the fringe of strawberry-blonde hair hanging down over her forehead. "Hey, if you're gettin' too old, what does that make me? A hag?"

Jackson's gaze went to the V of Audrey's blouse where the rounded curves of her breasts pushed up. "Far from it, baby."

She tapped his hand. "Hey, the eyes are up here."

A grin stretched Jackson's lips wide, and he glanced up into Audrey's baby-blue eyes. "I know that, but the view was better where I was at."

"Jerk." Despite her word, her eyes danced.

A customer leaned against the bar and ordered two whisky shooters. Audrey turned to the array of bottles lining the wall behind the bar and reached for the brand of whisky the man had asked for. No skinny minny, Audrey had a curvy ass encased in skin-hugging, washed-out jeans. An ass a man could get his hands on.

Jackson's groin tightened. Now here was a real woman, the kind he could sink his...er...teeth into.

Audrey's snug jeans molded to the curve of her butt and thighs, narrowing down the length of her long, beautiful legs to tuck neatly into go-to-hell, bright red cowboy boots, which sported diamond-shaped metal studs. She wore those boots just about everywhere.

Born and raised in the Texas panhandle, Audrey knew what Jackson knew—the only way to get what you wanted was to work hard and maybe break a few well-chosen rules along the way. And she'd done just that to get this bar started. Modeled after the Coyote Ugly bar in New York City, Audrey had hired only the pretty waitresses who could dance, some who could sing and all of which could sling drinks like a pro. As a side, she provided strippers, both male and female, for private parties, bachelorette parties and special occasions.

Tough but fair is what each of her girls would say about her. And the tips were good, so none of them complained about Audrey's hard-line approach. And to think, Audrey had accomplished all that in her twenties. She'd beat Jackson to thirty last year, celebrating her birthday with the two-year anniversary of the Ugly Stick Saloon. It had been a big blowout party with a live band, cheap beer and free rides home to those who couldn't drive themselves.

She had this bar-owner thing down like it was second nature. Some men found it intimidating. Jackson thought Audrey was sexy as hell. He'd toyed with the idea of asking her out, only to talk himself out of it too many times to count, always waiting for the right moment, the right situation. That right moment had never happened. Now, it felt like he'd missed his chance.

With a sigh, he turned to stare at his younger brothers. Maybe after they settled down, Jackson could get a life of his own. He'd been responsible for them ever since their parents died in an auto accident back when he'd been a senior in college. Mark and Luke had been fifteen years old at the time. Jackson had barely turned twenty-one when he'd stepped into his father's shoes to run the ranch and finish raising the twins.

At twenty-four, Mark and Luke showed no signs of slowing down. If anything, they were speeding up. He couldn't blame them for wanting to have fun. Hell, had he been this carefree at their age, he'd have been dancing with every young thing in the bar. Probably taking one home for a little...

A long, curvy drink of water slipped in front of him, her red boots tapping to the beat of the music. "Hey, cowboy, you gonna ask me to dance, or do I have to ask you?" Audrey grabbed his hand and tugged him toward the dance floor.

Jackson slipped from the barstool and allowed her to drag him along, even though he wasn't so sure he *wanted* to have fun. Where could it lead? "I haven't had enough to drink."

Audrey tossed her hair and shot a saucy grin his way. "Good, I didn't want you walkin' all over my good boots."

He swung her into his arms and eased them into the crowd moving in a wide circle around the dance floor. The music transitioned to a slow country waltz, and half of the couples used it as an opportunity to rest and get another drink.

AUDREY CLOSED HER EYES, letting her body feel the music. She melted against Jackson, her body pressing into his. What would it take to get the man to notice her as someone other than the owner of this bar? She'd flashed her boobs, given him a face-full of ass and now she rubbed her body against his from knee to shoulder. The man had to be dead or gay not to get the hint.

Did she have to throw herself at him and ask him to take her to bed? Damn it, she hadn't gotten laid in over a year, and the battery on her vibrator had died the night before. What else was a girl to do? All she wanted was a little relief here. *Hello.*

Her hands slipped around his waist and down into the back pockets of his jeans. She'd much rather be touching skin, but dancing was the closest she'd come to having sex in a long time. She'd been eyeing Jackson Gray Wolf for months, wondering what it would take to get him into her bed.

Both of them had been too busy with their own businesses to take the time out to relax and engage in a little nooky. Her thirtieth birthday had come and gone, and the death of her fourth set of vibrator batteries had her practically frothing at the mouth and other places farther south.

About the time Audrey began to think the man just wasn't into her, Jackson's fingers moved along her spine, spanning her waist, sliding down over her bottom to cup her ass. He pulled her up against the thick ridge of his cock, which pressed against the metal rivets of his jeans.

"Ummm. That's more like it." She laid her head on his chest, the steady beat of his heart thump-thumping in her ear. Or was that the bass drum, tapping in time to the music? Whatever, it felt good.

He slipped a hand up her side, his thumb brushing beneath her breast. "Is it hot in here, or is it me?"

"Baby, it's definitely you," Audrey said. "Want to get some air? I could use a break."

"Sounds good."

As Jackson pulled away from Audrey, she

wondered if she'd made the right decision. Outside, there wouldn't be enough noise and confusion to mask her blatant attempt to flirt with the man. Good Lord, why did she care? Every man and woman old enough to hold a liquor bottle in this county knew Audrey Anderson could hold her own in a bar and in a fight. Most would say she had the confidence of a prizefighter.

And when it came to the Ugly Stick Saloon, her confidence was hard-earned and recognized by even the worst of the roughest rednecks.

When it came to relationships, she sucked. Most men were intimidated by her forthrightness and straight talk. Some were turned off by it. Part of that was the act she put on. Part of it was her own hesitation. The last long-term relationship she'd been in had turned into a mess. He'd wanted to dominate her to the point of beating her.

Audrey wasn't putting up with that ever again. Still, part of her liked a man with a firm hand. Just not a heavy hand. Thus the long dry spell. She'd toyed with the idea of going lesbian until Jackson Gray Wolf caught her eye. But the only man who had interested her in the least hadn't shown any indication of wanting to have sex with her. Well, now was her chance to see if he'd consider it, or if he truly was immune to her.

She led the way toward the exit when Charli, her assistant manager and lead bartender, snagged her arm. "Audrey, we're out of Johnnie Walker Whisky up front, and I can't find that case we'd ordered in the storeroom."

Audrey swallowed her frustration and spoke calmly. "Get Libby to find it."

"She's filling in for a waitress on break, and there are ten people at the bar hollerin' for drinks. I could use a little help here."

Audrey sighed, casting an apologetic smile at Jackson. "Stay, follow or just forget it, I have to get this." She veered off toward the storeroom, her steps eating the distance. If Jackson stayed put, would he be there when she got back? Or would he leave, bored with the whole idea of stepping outside with her?

Pulling a ring of keys from her jeans pocket, she opened the storeroom and switched on the light. The whisky Charli needed was perched on the top shelf. Audrey hooked the step stool with her foot, dragged it toward the shelf and climbed up, sliding the heavy box of whisky toward her. She teetered, the weight causing her to lean backward more than she'd expected.

A large, solid palm attached itself to her butt, bracing her from falling.

"Let me get that." Jackson's hand moved from her ass to the box over her head, lifting it from her fingers.

Greta Sue, one of Audrey's best bouncers, stepped into the doorway, her linebacker body filling the entrance. "Charli said you'd have some whisky for her."

"Right here." Audrey ducked beneath Jackson's arm, grabbed the heavy box from him and handed it to the bouncer. "Take this to Charli. I'll be out there to help in a minute."

"Yes, ma'am." After Greta Sue left, Audrey stood with her back to Jackson, her pulse slowly returning to normal. "I guess I'd better get back to work."

She only took one step before Jackson hooked her arm and pulled her back into the storeroom. He kicked shut the door, spun her to face him and then backed her against the wood panel.

Her heart pounding, her vocal cords locking in her throat, Audrey stared up into the midnight-black, smoldering eyes of the Kiowa Indian. Every one of the Gray Wolf brothers had the signature hair and eyes, blacker than the night, and broad shoulders that filled any room they entered. But only Jackson captured her attention and held it so tightly she could barely breathe. He was strong, powerful and reeking of male testosterone. She wanted him to command her, to force her to submit to his every desire.

Audrey fought to regain her breath, bad memories rising to the surface. Suddenly she felt the need to run before she did something she might regret, like fall for the guy. "I really should be getting back to work."

He planted a hand against the door, effectively

blocking any attempt on her part to escape. His brawny arm stretched beside her, the sun-kissed skin smelling of the outdoors and leather. "Do you work all the time?"

Audrey's inner panic dissolved as her panties dampened, the stirrings of lust gripping her so strongly she couldn't shake it. "I could ask you the same thing." Was that really her voice, usually so strong and clear, now breathy and husky?

"I'm here, aren't I?" He brushed a strand of her hair away from her face and tucked it behind her ear.

"Only as designated driver to your brothers." She leaned her face into his hand. "They're adults now. You didn't have to come."

"And miss the opportunity to see you?"

Her eyes narrowed. "Since when did you care if you saw me?"

He inched closer, his lips hovering over hers, his knee pressing between her thighs. "Since forever."

"Liar." Audrey flattened her hands against his chest with the intent to push him away. Instead, her fingers curled, dragging him nearer by the fabric of his chambray shirt.

With his lips so near, Audrey couldn't think, couldn't breathe. When he didn't seal the kiss, she glanced up, her gaze meeting his.

"Has anyone ever told you that your eyes are as blue as a rain-washed summer sky?" His deep tone resonated against the cardboard boxes of liquor lining the storeroom walls.

Audrey laughed, her stomach fluttering, her knees turning to liquid. "No."

"Well, someone should. Because they are very beautiful." His mouth descended, crushing hers with the force of his kiss.

She gasped, her lips parting to allow him inside.

He swept past her teeth, delving deep to tangle and twist, thrusting in and out to the rhythm of lust. His fingers laced in her hair, tugging hard enough to make her scalp sting. The blasts of pain only made Audrey hotter.

Her thighs clenched around Jackson's knee, her cunt rubbing along the rough denim of his jeans. She ached with the need to be naked, to feel his skin against hers.

Jackson's lips left hers, burning a trail across her chin and along the convulsing column of her throat. With his free hand, he flipped the buttons loose from her blouse, shoving the edges over her shoulders and down her arms, exposing her favorite demi-bra, the thin black lace barely hiding her nipples. She whispered a silent prayer to the laundry gods for the piles of clothing she needed to wash, forcing her to wear her best bra and panties tonight.

Her shirt fell to the floor and her pulse shot into hyper-speed. This could be her lucky night. She could actually get laid and spare the batteries for once.

When Jackson reached for the rivet on her jeans, slipping it free and sliding the zipper down, Audrey almost shouted with joy. "Hurry," she said, afraid someone would catch them getting it on in the supply closet. Not that she cared about being caught, but she didn't want to waste a chance at what Jackson had to offer.

She loosened the four metal buttons on his jeans. His cock jutted free into her hand. It was longer, thicker and harder than any man Audrey had been with, one measure of proof to the rumor that American Indians were hung better than the average white man. He'd fill her to full and then some. Her pussy creamed in anticipation.

The race to naked intensified.

Jackson jerked her jeans and panties down her legs.

Audrey toed her boots, unable to slip them easily off her feet. With her jeans around her ankles, she couldn't step forward or lift a leg to get her boots off. She bent over and struggled with the red leather, cursing her once-favorite pair of cowboy boots for the nuisance they now were. With her bare ass in the air, she felt the cool draft of air-conditioning waft across her pussy.

A pair of strong, coarse hands smoothed over her hips and gripped her bottom, steadying her as she pulled one boot off. As she worked with the other boot, the hands moved, a finger sliding between her cheeks, finding and poking into her anus.

Her head jerked up and connected with Jackson's chin. Pain shot through her skull, and she almost fell to the ground with her legs still trapped in her jeans and one boot.

Jackson staggered backward, one hand cupping his chin, his eyes watering. A smile teased the corners of his lips.

"If you laugh, so help me..." Her own mouth turned up at the corners and before she could help herself, a chuckle rose up her throat. She leaned her back against the door. "Do you get the feeling we're destined to never do this?"

The laughter died in his eyes. "No." Jackson bent and pulled the other boot from her foot, sliding the jeans and panties over her ankles and feet.

Finally, she stood naked in front of him, her nipples pebbling in the cool air, her body so hot she thought she'd spontaneously combust.

And he stared at her, still fully clothed except for his cock jutting out of his fly.

When she should have been self-conscious, Audrey couldn't find the modesty necessary to even blush, her cheeks and body filling with a heat that had nothing to do with embarrassment. The way Jackson's coal-black gaze raked over her left her panting and ready for more than just a look.

Jackson pulled her against him, his penis pressing into her belly. He kissed her, then seared a path down to her breasts, taking one into his mouth, nipping at the beaded nipple and sucking it full into his mouth.

Audrey's leg curled around the back of Jackson's calf, sliding upward until her heal dug into his buttocks, her pussy rubbing against his penis. "Oh, please, do me."

He chuckled against her breast. "Do you?"

"Now, cowboy. Do it now."

"A man likes to make the calls."

"Then make it, damn it!"

"Shut up, woman, you're about to be fucked." Jackson's hands circled her buttocks, dropping low to clasp the backs of her thighs. Then he lifted her, settling her around his waist, his penis poised at her entrance.

"Wait." Audrey's legs clenched around him, holding her off his magnificent cock, every ounce of longing pushing her downward. "Please tell me you have a condom. Please."

Jackson froze, his face tense, his hands gripping her bottom so tightly, there'd be bruises. "My back pocket. Check my wallet."

She reached around him and dug in his back pocket, pulling his wallet free. She flipped it open and rifled through the contents. Credit cards, dollars, driver's license and one lonely foil package, buried beneath it all.

"Oh, thank God." She shoved the wallet back into his pocket and tore the package open with her teeth.

Jackson leaned her back against the door as she sheathed him, rolling the ribbed condom down over his cock, its tight fit only making her more determined to get him inside her soon.

With the condom in place, her passion waning

only slightly, Audrey settled her arms across Jackson's shoulders and eased herself down over him, taking him fully into her channel. "Oh, baby, fuck me. Fuck me hard."

He grinned. "Ah, the lady likes it rough."

"You have no idea," she whispered against his lips.

He pressed her against the cool paneling of the door and slammed into her, driving deep and hard. With each thrust, the door banged, the sound echoing through the storeroom. The light bulb dangling from the ceiling swayed, and the world could have stopped for all Audrey cared. She was getting what she wanted, and she didn't have to change the batteries to get there.

The pounding on the door changed tempos from the rhythm Jackson set.

It wasn't long before shouts penetrated the wood. "Audrey? Audrey, are you in there?" Charli's voice sounded high-pitched and desperate on the other side.

Jackson froze in mid-thrust, his eyes widening.

"Fuck!" Audrey swore, her legs clasping Jackson to her, drawing him deep. "I swear I'm going to fire her."

"Are you okay in there?" Charli banged on the door again. "Audrey, answer if you can. Otherwise we're going to break down the door."

Audrey leaned her forehead into Jackson's chest. "Just when we were getting to the good part," she whispered. Aloud, she called out, "I'm fine. Go away."

"Not until I know you're okay."

"I'm okay."

"Show me. For all I know someone could be holding a gun to your head."

"I'd like to hold a gun to *your* head," Audrey shouted.

"What? I can barely hear you." Charli pounded again. "Open the door."

"I'll be out in a minute."

Jackson lifted her off his cock and set her on the floor. "Maybe you're right. It wasn't meant to be." He peeled the condom off his dick and tucked his long staff into his jeans before buttoning the fly.

"Yeah." Audrey sighed, gathering her scattered clothing. "I better get back to work."

"Look, Audrey—"

"Don't." She pressed her fingers to his lips. "Don't say it was a mistake. I know it."

"That's not what I was going to say."

"Well, save it." She shoved her feet into her jeans and pulled her cowboy boots on.

"Audrey?" Charli's muffled shout made Audrey's blood pressure rocket.

"I'm coming, dammit." She hooked her bra in place and slid her arms into her shirt, making quick work of the buttons. Charli's interruption had probably saved Audrey from a big mistake. What the business needed should always come first. Her own personal wants and desires were secondary. The business needed her to remain respectable. Which meant no jacking around with a Kiowa hottie in the storeroom.

With a lopsided smile, she paused with her hand on the doorknob. "Thanks anyway."

Jackson's jaw tightened, his lips pressing into a straight line. "This isn't over."

"As far as I'm concerned it is." When she opened the door, Charli stood there, her eyes wide and worried.

"Oh, thank God." She hugged Audrey tight. "I thought you were being held hostage. The boys were going to break down the door to get you out."

Behind her, Mark and Luke stood, grins spreading across their faces as soon as they spotted Jackson.

Mark tipped his cowboy hat. "Just here to help." He nodded toward the bottom of Audrey's shirt. "You missed a button."

Luke jabbed him in the ribs. "Glad everything's okay. We'll just be...er...goin'." He jerked Mark by the arm, dragging him away from the storeroom.

Charli's eyes rounded and her face turned a brilliant shade of red. "Were you two...? Did I...?" She ducked her head and retreated. "I'll be bartending."

Audrey sighed. It was just as well Charli had interrupted before things got out of hand. She wasn't certain she could have extricated herself from Jackson easily, and she knew nothing could come of a continued liaison with the cowboy. All she wanted was a quick fuck. Jackson didn't strike her as a fuck-'em-and-leave-'em type. She had her bar, which was more work than even she'd envisioned and frankly, she wasn't ready for commitment of any kind—wasn't sure she'd ever be ready to trust another man with her heart or her body.

CHAPTER TWO

"*A*bsolutely no birthday party this year. Agreed?" Surly, and in no mood for civilized company, Jackson had his brothers lined up outside the barn, ready to rip into them.

Mark snorted. "What's the matter, Jack? Feeling a little cranky this morning? Age getting to you?"

"Would be just fine if I didn't have to babysit the two of you. And no changing the subject. I want a promise from the both of you. You're not going to throw a big party for my thirtieth, are you?" His eyes narrowed. "I can't hear you," he said in his best drill-sergeant imitation.

Mark and Luke snapped to attention, popping their brother a mock salute. "Yes, sir! No big party, sir!"

For a long moment Jackson glared at them. They'd agreed far too quickly, but he wasn't up to knocking sense into them. Not when his jeans rubbed against his cock, reminding him of what he hadn't finished last night and the aching need it had kindled in his groin. The more he thought about it, the more he wanted to hit someone. If he didn't get away from his twin brothers, he'd start there. "The northernmost fence has a wire snapped. You two get it fixed and start work on replacing those boards on the cattle chute near the highway. The truck comes tomorrow to load the steers. We can't wait until the last minute to shore up."

"I'll get the barbed wire." Mark strode into the barn to retrieve the wire stacked in the storeroom.

"I've got the tools." Luke patted a cloth bag of tools.

"Four-wheelers?" Mark returned, carrying a roll of wire.

Luke nodded. "You bet." Then he turned to Jackson. "Don't forget that cow with the infected udder."

Jackson forced a smile he didn't really feel. Despite his surliness, Jackson was proud of the boys. When his younger brothers got down to business, they didn't waste time. "I'll be out rounding up ol' Betsy and her calf and bringing them in for the vet to take a look."

"Sure you aren't the one who needs help?" Luke asked.

Jackson shook his head. "It'll take both of you to get that chute in shape in a single day. I can handle one cow."

Mark cast a glance at Luke, his brows raised.

"Better him than me. Betsy got the better of me once. Got the scar to prove it." He patted his right rib cage.

Luke slapped Mark on the back. "Don't care to repeat the humiliation?"

Mark snorted. "Nope."

"Then let's get going. We have a lot to do today." Luke glanced at Jackson. "Mark and I will cook dinner tonight, so don't be late for birthday cake."

Jackson didn't want to remember his birthday, and his brothers seemed bent on reminding him that he was another year older. He could go the rest of his life without birthday cake and be perfectly happy. "Don't bother." Thankful for any excuse to avoid a birthday dinner and the inevitable birthday cake, he delighted in announcing, "I gotta go to town and make a deposit at the bank, and afterward Charli asked me to stop by."

Mark grinned. "Got a hot date?"

Jackson shook his head, an image of Audrey, not Charli, standing naked in the soft light of the store-room, making his dick twitch. But it wasn't Audrey he'd be paying a visit. "No date. Charli wanted me to bring a ladder and change a light bulb she can't reach over the entryway." He didn't bother to explain that the entryway was over the back door of the Ugly Stick Saloon. Maybe he'd catch Audrey on break and pick up where they'd left off.

His brothers smirked and high-fived each other. Okay, so they had it half right. Jackson needed sex, but not with Charli.

"The old light-bulb excuse, is it?" Mark chuckled.

Jackson's eyes narrowed as he feigned ignorance. "What do you mean?"

"Nothing." Luke jammed an elbow into Mark's gut. "Come on, we should be making hay while the sun shines."

Jackson squeezed his eyes shut and pinched the bridge of his nose. "When are you two going to grow up?"

"Never," Mark answered. "Especially if it means we'll be as ornery and frustrated as you, big brother."

"No kidding," Luke added. "You've been so busy being more of a father to the two of us, you haven't had time to live your own life. Face it, old man, we're all grown up and you need a woman in your life."

Mark snorted. "What he needs is to get laid."

"What I need is the two of you to quit lollygaggin' and get to work." Jackson's words came across harsh. What gave his brothers the right to tell him what he needed? He'd been the head of the household long enough to know his own mind. But damned if Luke's words didn't strike a little too close to home.

"Point made. He's not getting any and it shows." Luke leaped out of the way of Jackson's fist. "Getting slower too."

"Age must be catching up to him," Mark agreed.

He and Luke ran for the four-wheelers, laughing.

Luke glanced back, all humor wiped from his face. "Think about it." Then he gunned the engine and shot off for the north fence.

Unfortunately, that left Jackson feeling older than his thirty years and in no mood to put up with a stubborn cow with udder problems. Three hours later, he was hot, sweaty and dusty and had Betsy penned in a stall, her calf bawling in the corral outside the barn. Each time the calf wailed, the cow sent an answering moo until Jackson thought his head would split from the noise.

Doc Richards arrived in his pickup, unloaded his doctoring bag and set to work treating the cow's udder with disinfectants and antibiotic ointment. After administering a shot of antibiotics, the vet gathered his things and stuck out his hand to Jackson. "By the way, happy birthday."

Jackson grimaced. "How'd you find out?"

"Your brothers made a point of telling anyone who'd listen last night at the Ugly Stick."

"Great. They had better not be throwing a party this year. For one, I won't be there."

Doc grinned. "If they are, I didn't get an invite."

"Good." Jackson thought better of his answer. "Not that I wouldn't want you there. I just don't want a party. Too much hoopla over nothin'."

"A man only turns thirty once."

"And any other birthday is different?"

The veterinarian shrugged. "Guess not, but I'd give my right arm to be thirty again."

"It's just another day, as far as I'm concerned."

"Leigh Ann and I celebrated our second anniversary and had our first child the year I turned thirty."

The veterinarian stared off into the distance. "Yeah, that was a good year." His gaze shifted to Jackson. "Well, happy birthday, anyway. Each year is what you make of it, I always say." He clapped Jackson on the back and climbed into his truck.

Jackson usually enjoyed seeing Doc Richards, but after the man left, he found himself in an even deeper funk than before he'd come. As he moved ol' Betsy back out in the pasture to be with her calf, the ungrateful beast snagged him with her horn, ripping his favorite denim shirt. The day hadn't started in the right direction and only seemed to be going downhill from there.

The twins hadn't made it back from working on the cattle chute by late afternoon, giving Jackson all the time he needed to take care of the chores around the barn, feed the horses, cows and chickens and check on the garden. By the time he was finished, showered and changed into clean jeans, the sun had dipped below the horizon, casting the landscape into a dusky shadow. He might get off the ranch before the boys could razz him more about turning thirty.

"Damned birthdays. Who needs 'em anyway?" he muttered as he climbed into his pickup and slammed the door. He might stay out all night just to avoid Mark and Luke and their well-intentioned annoyance.

Jackson swung by the barn, loaded the ladder in the bed of the truck and turned to the north. Dust rose against the fading light in the distance, indicating his brothers' return from the range. The sooner Jackson left, the better. He hopped up into the truck, shifted into drive and spit up gravel from his tires as he tore out of the barnyard.

After stopping to make a night deposit at the bank in Hole in the Wall, Jackson headed out the other end of town, his headlights the only ones shining on the road as the hour grew late.

The closer he got to the bar, the more he got to thinkin'. What if Charli's request was some elaborate setup to get him to come to a surprise party?

His foot hit the brake and the truck skidded to a stop in the middle of the highway.

No way. He wasn't falling for that. Thirty was too round a figure for his brothers to let it slide. This had to be a setup.

His foot eased off the brake. Then again, if it wasn't a ploy to get him to the saloon, and he didn't show up, Charli and Audrey would have to exit work in the middle of the night in the dark.

Jackson eased his foot onto the accelerator. He'd sneak into the back parking lot, change the bulb and be gone before anyone saw him. And before he saw anyone else—including Audrey.

His groin tightened, the storeroom calling to him, Audrey's delectable body more than he could resist. Okay, so maybe he'd see if she wanted to ditch the bar and go out for a cup of coffee with him. Maybe they could take their coffee out by the lake and…

Before he knew it, Jackson was speeding toward

the Ugly Stick Saloon located on the county line between Hole in the Wall and Temptation, Texas. He didn't realize he'd exceeded the speed limit until he passed one of the local Texas State Troopers with a radar gun pointed in his direction.

Immediately, his foot left the accelerator and he brought the truck and his rampant lust in check, arriving at the Ugly Stick in a more sedate mood and at a slower pace.

He ducked low, hoping no one would recognize him. Fat chance. The place was already swinging, country music shaking the corrugated tin walls of the building. In places as small as Hole in the Wall and Temptation, everyone knew everyone and the horse they rode in on—or what car or truck they drove. Jackson did his best to round the back of the saloon before anyone noticed his arrival.

Feeling confident he'd gone unnoticed, Jackson removed the ladder from the back of his truck and set it up outside the back door. In less than two minutes he'd changed the light bulb and reloaded the ladder, ready to go home.

At this point he had choices.

He could leave, no one the wiser of his visit, possibly avoiding a surprise party and the embarrassment of everyone at the Ugly Stick congratulating him on reaching the ripe old age of thirty with nothing to show for it. Yeah, he had the same ranch. Still had the same work. No wife, no kids to brag about, and the only sex he'd had in months was stolen in the back of the storeroom of this saloon the night before. And that hadn't really counted because they'd been interrupted before either one of them had a chance to come.

Pathetic.

He opened the truck and had his foot on the running board when he thought again of that storeroom, Audrey and his other choice.

Jackson could stay. Maybe the party wasn't all that big. Audrey would be there to keep the drunks from tearing her building down. They might sneak back into that storeroom, lock the door and finish what they'd started the night before.

His foot dropped to the ground and he sighed. He wanted to see Audrey, but what was the chance they'd get it on again? She'd called their tryst in the storeroom a mistake.

The only mistake Jackson figured was unlocking the door.

Situating his jeans to fit more comfortably around his ever-swelling cock, Jackson closed the truck door, locked it and headed into the Ugly Stick, ready to test the waters with the owner, determined to convince the woman that what they'd done was nowhere near a mistake and only the beginning.

"WHAT DO you mean CJ's sick? Hell, I didn't even know we had a request for tonight. Who the hell am I gonna find at this short notice?" Audrey shook the payment receipt in the air.

Charli flipped through the black book of phone numbers Audrey kept by the desk in the office of the Ugly Stick Saloon. "I don't know. I've called all the other girls and they're either out of town or on other gigs."

"What about Kendall? She's old enough now."

"Out of town."

Audrey's eyes narrowed. "What about you?"

Charli held up her hands. "No way. I'm a singer. I can't dance to save my life."

"Seriously, Charli, how much dancing do you have to do? You just shake your boobs and ass and make the birthday boy happy."

"I told you when I started here I wasn't going to dance. And I wasn't supposed to work tonight, as it is, but with the rodeo in town…"

Audrey ran a hand through her hair, pushing it back away from her face. "Who am I going to get to do this? Hell, who's it for?" She squinted at the receipt, turning it sideways. "Is this your writing?"

"Yes." Charli grabbed the document from her. "It's for the Gray Wolf twins."

Heat pooled between Audrey's thighs. "When did you take this order?"

"Last night. I had CJ all lined up and then she called me this afternoon claiming she's sick."

"Can't she dance sick?"

Charli frowned at Audrey. "Not when it's food

poisoning or stomach flu." She shook her head. "Besides, you don't want your paying customers to catch whatever she's got. The Gray Wolf twins promised it would be a small number at the party, three people tops."

Audrey crossed her arms over her chest. "Who is the party for?"

Her assistant's lips twisted. "I think they planned on surprising Jackson with a stripper for his thirtieth birthday."

"I heard him threatening them if they even hinted at a party last night. How did they manage to get this one by him?"

"Umm…while you had him otherwise occupied, they spoke with me." Charli refused to meet Audrey's eyes.

Audrey smelled something fishy and crossed her arms over her chest. "CJ isn't sick, is she?"

Charli stared over Audrey's shoulder. "Uh…well…"

"You didn't even call her, did you?"

"Well…uh…" Charli tapped the receipt against her cheek. "Not really."

"Either you did or you didn't. Fess up or you're fired."

"In that case…" Charli grimaced. "Didn't."

"And you've promised the Gray Wolf twins a stripper?"

"Kinda."

"Not kinda. I have a receipt in my hand." Audrey

shook the paper at Charli. "You promised it, you deliver. I'll have nothing to do with it." She turned and hefted a case of whisky from the corner of her desk, in need of some manual labor to burn off her anger. "I'm not going to be hoodwinked into dancing for Jackson Gray Wolf."

"But, Audrey, you're the best dancer at the Ugly Stick." Charli followed her down the hallway to the storeroom.

"I gave up my dancing shoes when I bought this dump."

"And you've made it even better and more profitable in the past two years, sacrificing your own personal life to do it."

Audrey shoved the case of booze onto a shelf and spun. "Oh, so now you're telling me my personal life sucks?"

"No, I wouldn't...well...okay, yes I would." Charli fisted her hands and planted them on her hips. "You've been grumpy and witchy for the past couple of weeks, and it would do good for you to get out and have a little fun."

"And dancing for the Gray Wolf clan is your idea of fun?" Audrey maintained the angry look on her face even as warmth spread from her core throughout her body as images of the sexy Native Americans flitted through her mind. Dancing nearly naked in front of them...no...*him*...had her body burning almost as hot as it had the night before when she'd been completely naked in the storeroom with

Jackson. Sweet Jesus, what would it be like to have all three?

Audrey swallowed hard, strengthening her resolve. She had set aside her own needs while building the Ugly Stick into a viable establishment, offering the best in entertainment and drinks this side of Austin. She'd sunk every bit of her hard-earned savings into the place, banking on its success. Failure wasn't an option and fooling around with the hottest men in the tri-county area wasn't either.

Charli pushed. "If I could dance, I'd do it in a heartbeat. Think about having all three of those men staring at you, admiring your body..." She sighed. "You never know what could come of such a sexy private party. I'd love to find out, but I just can't make it tonight, and the most important point—I can't dance." Her dreamy look faded and hardened into a more serious, businesslike demeanor. "I'll just have to call and cancel. I can refund the five hundred dollars they paid."

"Five hundred dollars?" Audrey stared down at the number on the receipt. "Why five hundred? We usually charge half of that."

"Short notice." Charli grinned. "I made them pay."

"You bitch." Audrey couldn't help the smile lifting the corners of her lips, but immediately reined it in. "That still doesn't resolve the issue of who will provide the entertainment."

"Audrey, you have to." Charli took the receipt

from Audrey's fingers. "Aren't you the one who always says we can't disappoint our customers?"

"You were the one who made the appointment, you figure it out."

"You're right. I shouldn't have gotten you involved. I'll call and cancel." Charli turned and headed for the office, the receipt in her hands, her head down.

Audrey's gaze followed. Part of her wanted to say, *Damned right!* But the part that had been with Jackson last night in the storeroom wanted to dance for the Gray Wolf brothers. But how could she when she was trying to establish herself as an upstanding business-woman in a small town? She hadn't danced since she'd bought the Ugly Stick, trying to play down her reputation as a stripper ever since. Hell, the towns-people had only just started speaking to her while staring into her eyes, not down her cleavage.

Then again, her batteries were dead in her vibrator and she hadn't had a decent orgasm in...oh hell, too long to remember.

"Wait." Audrey hurried after Charli and caught her as she completed punching in numbers on the telephone.

"What?" Charli stared up at Audrey, all innocence.

"We'll do it, damn it." Audrey ripped the phone out of Charli's hands and set it in the cradle. "But don't ever pull this crap on me again. I won't be manipulated."

Charli's face split into a grin. "I promise. I just knew you were the right person for this gig."

"Not me. I have someone else in mind." An idea had begun to blossom, and she turned away before Charli could guess what it was. "I know just the right person to do this job, and she's available."

Charli grasped her arm, spinning her around. "But that's not…"

Audrey stared down at Charli's hand. "Not what, Charli?"

"Not what…I had in mind."

"What did you have in mind?" Audrey pursed her lips.

"You."

"Well, it's not going to be Audrey Anderson strutting her stuff in front of the Gray Wolf brothers. She hung up her dancing shoes when she purchased the Ugly Stick. Besides, I have someone better in mind."

"But—"

Audrey gave Charli what she hoped was a withering look. "But what?"

Charli's face scrunched as if dodging a hit. "Did I mention they wanted someone willing to throw in a little kink?"

"Kink?" A shiver of unwanted excitement skittered across Audrey's skin. "What do you mean kink?"

"I don't know, maybe a little sub and Dom action."

"Just who gets to be the sub?" Audrey planted her

fists on her hips, looking anything but submissive, while inside her body quivered.

The other woman clamped her lips shut, her forehead wrinkled in a worried frown. "That part is optional of course. Don't worry. I'm sure they'll be happy with just a dance."

"They'll have to be, because that's all they're gonna get." Audrey shook her head. Charli had gone way past the limit this time. She'd have to have a long talk with the girl when this was all over. "You'll have to cover the bar tonight, this might take some finagling." And she was just the finagler to do it. A plan formed in her mind that would fulfill a company promise, satisfy her sexual frustration and keep her reputation intact. It was a big order to fill, but one she could do if she played her cards right.

Self-doubt hit her as soon as she skipped out the front door of the bar.

Had it been too long? Had she forgotten everything in the past two years? Could she get away with it and not get caught? Audrey's heartbeat skipped into overdrive as she climbed into her bright red pickup and headed to her little house on the edge of Temptation.

Tonight she'd get what she wanted and give the Gray Wolf men what they wanted and walk away string-free—no commitment, no one maintaining control over her.

Win-win!

CHAPTER THREE

*W*hen Jackson entered through the back door of the Ugly Stick Saloon, he braced himself against the loud music and the potential of even louder screams of *Surprise!*

Instead Charli stepped in his path before he'd gotten five feet inside the door. "Jackson. Just the man I was thinking about." Charli's laugh was a little more high-pitched than usual. She hooked his arm, dragged him through the Ugly Stick and pushed him toward a barstool, shooting a furtive glance over her shoulder at the bar entrance. "Can I get you a drink?"

He frowned, his gaze roving over the bar, the dance floor and the patrons already seated at the tables. A few of the regulars lifted a hand or nodded in his direction. "I didn't plan on staying." So where was the party? The only surprise he had was the niggle of disappointment he felt that no one pounded him on the back, congratulating him on reaching his thirtieth birthday.

"Oh, come on, just one drink. Then you can fix that light bulb that's blown out in the back entryway." Charli scooted around to the other side of the bar.

"Already replaced it." Jackson hesitated, then slipped onto the barstool.

"Oh. Well, then have a drink on the house for fixing our light." She grabbed a tall beer mug and filled it from the tap, her movements jerky, almost nervous, if Jackson wasn't mistaken.

"Something wrong?" he asked.

"What could possibly be wrong?" She slapped the beer on the counter, sloshing liquid over the sides. "Oops." With an apologetic grin, she grabbed a rag and sopped up the beer.

Jackson snagged her wrist, rag and all. "Hey, it's me. Why are you so nervous?"

"No reason." She gave him a smile so fake, Jackson thought her lips would crack. "None whatsoever." Charli untangled her wrist from his grip and moved out of reach. "Excuse me. I have to get something from the back."

"Is Audrey working tonight?" Jackson asked and lifted his beer to his lips, feigning a nonchalance he didn't feel.

"No." Charli grinned. "No, she's got another commitment." The woman disappeared into the back room.

His hands wrapped around the cool beer mug,

Jackson stared down into the frothy liquid. No party, just as he'd asked. The sense of satisfaction wasn't all he'd thought it would be. The fact that Audrey wasn't there had more do with it than the lack of celebration, and the thought of Audrey's other *commitment* made him grind his teeth.

The swelling in his groin hadn't dissipated much from the previous night, leaving him more twitchy and frustrated than before. Worse still, he didn't have a hope of alleviating his need in the very near future.

He downed the rest of the beer and set the mug on the counter. He had to get out of there, maybe take a drive with the windows down to cool off. He could swing by Audrey's place, if he knew where that was. She'd said something about living in Temptation.

Nah, she'd think he was stalking her, and Jackson didn't want her to think he was that desperate.

Hell, he might as well go home and hit the sack. There was plenty of work the next day to wear him out. Living on a ranch, he never lacked for something to keep him busy—always a fence to mend, an animal needing attention, equipment to fix, not to mention a herd of steers to load onto a tractor-trailer rig.

Jackson left the bar and climbed into his truck. Driving away, he glanced back at the Ugly Stick and shook his head. He couldn't believe his brothers really didn't plan anything for him. And many of his friends had been at the bar, which meant no party awaiting his return to the house.

With a sigh, Jackson shifted into drive and headed for the ranch, to slog through the last couple hours of his birthday, unnoticed, uncelebrated and completely uneventful. Just as he'd asked.

What had his mother always said?

Careful what you wish for, you might just get it.

Thirty minutes later, he arrived at the ranch house, pulling up beside his brother's trucks, the only other vehicles in the driveway.

He sat for a minute, studying the house.

The television was on in the living room, the light from the monitor glowing through the open blinds.

Mark rose from the couch and walked past the window into the hallway, returning a minute later with a bowl. Probably popcorn. A typical night at the Gray Wolf house. Boring. Uneventful.

Confident he wasn't facing a gauntlet of well-wishers, Jackson entered the house.

"Hey, Jackson, how was your hot date?" Luke called out without budging from his position sprawled across one end of the couch.

"It wasn't a date. I changed a light bulb." Jackson peeked around the corner of the hallway into the kitchen. No one waited in the shadows to jump out and surprise him.

"Looking for something?" Mark stepped up behind him.

"No. Just making sure someone cleaned up the kitchen."

"We got that covered." Mark opened the door to

the refrigerator. "I grilled a steak for you if you're still hungry."

"No thanks. I think I'll hit the sack. Got a lot to do tomorrow."

"Suit yourself." Mark returned to the living room without further comment.

That's it? Had his brothers actually complied with his wishes for the first time ever? Jackson smiled as he headed toward his room, the smile fading the closer he got to his door. Turning thirty had been a completely normal day. So much so, it left him feeling a bit empty. If he wasn't mistaken, he'd say he was downright sad. No party, no Audrey. All he had to show for the day was one torn shirt and a doctored cow udder.

Jackson pulled his shirt over his head and sat on the side of his bed, toeing off his boots, one at a time, dropping them to the floor.

A loud thump and a shout sounded from the living room. What the heck were Mark and Luke up to at this hour? Weren't they getting a little old to wrestle in the house? Jackson listened and the noise stopped.

When he stood to unbutton his jeans, music filtered through his door. The sound built and swelled, thump, thump, thumping against the walls until Jackson could no longer ignore it. Anger surged through him as he shoved through his door and stomped down the hallway to the living room.

The couches had been pushed back against the

walls and all of the lights had been turned down or off except one lamp that had been stripped of its shade, the bulb replaced by a black-light bulb. A strobe light perched on the fireplace mantel blinked off and on, adding to the nightclub feel of the room.

Jackson came to a halt, nearly tripping over an ottoman when a lithe, graceful figure entered the room. Her long, straight, platinum-blonde hair swung down around her hips. A white cowboy hat and a Lone Ranger mask guarded her face from view. But it wasn't her face Jackson was looking at.

She wore a white blouse tied snuggly beneath her full, voluptuous breasts. Her bare midriff displayed taut abs all the way down to the tie strap of the leather chaps riding low on the sexy swell of her hips. Beneath the chaps she wore a white string-bikini bottom that glowed brightly. On her feet dark cowboy boots glistened with shiny metal diamond-shaped studs, sparkling in the flash of the strobe and black light.

His breath caught in his throat, Jackson stood transfixed as the woman strutted into the center of the room and stopped with her hands on her hips, her feet spread wide.

The music changed tempos to his favorite country-western song about saving horses and riding cowboys.

One boot tapped against the hardwood floor, then the other, the chaps swaying with the movement of the blonde's hips.

Jackson's mouth dried, his cock twitched and the pulse at the base of his throat pounded to the rhythm of the music.

Mark and Luke hooted and hollered, stomping their feet with the beat, jerking Jackson out of his trance. For a moment he'd been the only man in the room. Now he was one of three, ogling a dancer. Anger spurred by his mounting irritation pushed Jackson over the edge.

"What the hell's going on?" he shouted.

The music played on, and the dancer rocked her pelvis, her arms rising toward the ceiling. She rolled her head, the long bleached-blonde hair swishing down over her back. When she turned, Jackson groaned.

The back of the bikini bottom was nothing more than a thin strip of material disappearing down the crack of her ass. She bent over, giving him a full moon of two luscious butt cheeks.

"What does it look like?" Mark grinned and rose off the couch. "We hired a stripper in honor of your birthday, but since you didn't want any part of a party, we decided not to cancel. Someone ought to get a little enjoyment out of the money we spent."

Luke stood too and held out his hand to the dancer.

She placed her fingers in his and allowed him to twirl her away from him, then back into a tight clinch in his arms, his knee parting her thighs, her buttocks shining Jackson's way. The blonde's hips rocked, rubbing her pussy over Luke's thigh. She mashed her breasts against his chest.

Jackson closed his eyes and pushed a hand through his hair. This wasn't helping him at all. He wanted Audrey, not this blonde. But the woman had moves that were driving him wild with need.

"Is the music keeping you up, old man?" Mark reached out for the blonde's hand. "We can turn down the volume."

The woman tugged Mark close, sandwiching herself between the brothers. Her arms stretched out behind her, palms clamping down on Mark's ass, pressing his groin against her near-naked ass.

A jolt of electricity shot through Jackson, his dick rubbing hard against the buttons of his jeans.

"I'm Kiki." She lifted a hand toward him, beckoning, speaking for the first time, her voice low, husky and dripping with sensuality. "Don't you want to join us?"

His feet moved him forward a step before Jackson's brain engaged. "No. I don't do foursomes."

"That's too bad...because I do." She shrugged and traced a finger along the side of Luke's face, sliding lower to the length of his neck and down his chest where she flicked the buttons of his shirt open.

Jackson told himself to leave the room and let his brothers have their fun. He backed up a step with every intention of returning to his bedroom, maybe to a cold shower or two.

Kiki's tongue poked out of her mouth and slid

along her full, voluptuous lips. Her chin dipped and she shot a half smile at him, her light eyes shining through the black mask.

"Oh, come on, Jackson." Mark's hands rested on the woman's hips, rising slowly up her sides to cup her breasts. "Stick around for the show. Really, what's it going to hurt?"

What would it hurt? His balls and his dick, that's what. If he didn't get some relief soon, he'd bust the buttons on his jeans. Jackson resisted adjusting himself, refusing to let his brothers know how much their little stripper had him under her spell.

He forced his shoulders to relax enough to shrug. "I guess I'd better stick around and make sure you two don't make any unwanted advances."

Mark's hands slipped around Kiki's waist and down to the triangle of material. "Hey, sweetheart, let me know when my advances are unwanted."

"Oh, baby, I'm wanting." She clasped his hands and slid them inside the white fabric, leaning back against him, her head resting on his chest, exposing the long, sexy line of her neck.

Jackson staggered backward, his butt connecting with the arm of the sofa. He perched on the edge, promising himself he'd leave if the dancing got any more graphic. He'd never been one to watch while others fucked. It wasn't right.

The dancer reached out and flicked the buttons of her shirt open, loosening the knot beneath her breasts.

Behind her, Mark lifted the shirt from her shoulders, peeling it down her arms to her elbows. He stopped there and twisted the fabric behind her back.

Kiki's eyes widened, her lips forming into a pout. "But I can't move my arms."

Mark grinned. "Exactly. It was the kinky part we asked for."

Jackson half-rose from the couch, ready to intervene.

The blonde's eyelids drooped, a sexy smile curling the corners of her mouth. "Okay. So you like to play a little rough?"

"Oh, yeah, baby." Luke grabbed her hips, dragging her hard against him. "For a stripper, you're wearing too many clothes."

"Let me dance." She cast a glance over her shoulder at Mark. "I'll remedy that little problem."

Mark's brows dipped, his hand tightening on the fabric of the shirt clinching her arms together behind her. "I don't know. I kinda like the rough play. Perhaps my brother can help you with the rest of your stripping routine."

"Only if it's the other brother." She nodded toward Jackson.

"Uh-uh." Jackson crossed his arms over his naked chest. "I told you, I don't do foursomes."

"Come on, Jack. We want to see what else she has to offer," Luke begged.

"If he doesn't come out to play, I'm done for the

night." Kiki tilted her head toward Jackson in challenge.

"You gotta do it," Luke groaned. "What I'm feeling is amazing." His hand slipped lower, dipping between her thighs. "All wet and juicy. Damn it, Jackson, have a heart."

Jackson stood with every intention of leaving the room. But the eyes looking out from the black mask mesmerized him, drawing him closer.

"Please." She tugged against the shirt binding her arms behind her back.

"Not what I had in mind." With a slight frown, Mark relinquished his hold.

Kiki pulled her shirt back up her shoulders and stuck out a hand, her fingers long, tapered, the nails neatly trimmed and plain, no colored polish, just the way Jackson liked them.

Try as he might, he couldn't resist. As if of its own accord, his arm rose, his fingers clasping hers, letting her draw him into the circle of her sensuality. Damn, he'd never live this down with his brothers. But at the moment, he didn't care. He was fully under the stripper's magic charm.

AUDREY COULDN'T BELIEVE she was getting away with her charade. Her body burned, her pussy wet with her juices. Having Jackson watch as she strutted her stuff in front of his brothers had been so much of a turn-on, she'd broken most of her rules of stripping, and she was raring to break all the rest.

Luke let go of his grip on her pussy and backed up a step, allowing more room for big brother.

A thrill of adrenaline shot through Audrey, her core heating to molten hot. The twins were handsome with their dark Kiowa skin, high cheekbones and jet-black hair, and she wouldn't mind making love to both of them. At the same time. But Jackson...

She sucked in a long, deep breath and let it out slowly. This was a man's man. Strip him down to a loincloth and he'd fit right in with his ancestors, hunting buffalo, fighting wars and making love with his woman. His broad shoulders flashed in and out of the strobe, the light casting shadows, emphasizing the distinct muscular definition of his chest and arms.

Her gaze dropped to the top button of his jeans, flipped casually open as if he'd been in the process of undressing when she'd begun her little dance.

She drew him near and flicked the other three buttons from their bindings with quick, desperate strokes. As the last button poked through the hole, his cock sprang free, slipping easily into her palm.

"Knew you weren't immune to Kiki." Luke laughed. "Hey, Mark, check out that boner."

Jackson jerked back, sliding out of Audrey's grip.

Mark swung a wooden stool into the center of the floor and shoved Jackson toward it. "Sit. And no jerking off."

He sat and growled at his brothers, his hands going to his open fly and the shaft jutting straight upward.

Luke cranked the music volume up a notch and danced toward Audrey. "Now that you have the birthday boy in position, let me help you out of that shirt."

It wasn't what Audrey had in mind, but the angry frown on Jackson's face gave her the courage to taunt him more, show him what he was missing. A little foreplay was just what he needed to make him eager to join the fun.

Audrey tied the tails of her shirt beneath her breasts, a good start for a strip tease.

"Did I give you permission to dress?" Luke shook his head and stalked her. "You know what the Gray Wolfs do to naughty girls?"

Her body quivered as she backed away from Luke and into Mark's chest.

Jackson lunged forward.

"Down, boy." Luke clamped a hand on Jackson's shoulder and shoved him back on the seat. "You'll have your turn. We want to get her ready for you. This is your show, brought to you by the brothers Gray Wolf. Sit back and relax."

Jackson growled again, his arms crossing over his chest, hands fisted. "Relax…hmph."

Luke grabbed the lapels of Audrey's shirt and yanked it upward, extending Audrey's arms high over her head. There he twisted the fabric, knotting it tightly around her wrists. She stood in the bikini thong, chaps and her prettiest black lace demi-bra, her breasts pushed up, ripe for the tasting, should any man in the room care to go for it.

Audrey's skin stung where the shirt sleeves had scraped across, the slight pain even more titillating than she'd imagined. She wanted more. "Hey, what if I want to play too?" She tugged, but couldn't free her hands. As a woman who'd been in control for the past two years, she was struck by this new sensation. These men had her at their mercy, a place she'd rarely allowed herself to be. A place she'd sworn she'd never go to again. But damned if she didn't want more. She'd play along, just a little.

Luke wagged a finger at her. "We are the masters. You don't have a choice. Submit or suffer punishment."

Master. A wash of juices rushed through her pussy. Audrey had been submissive once. What had it bought her? Bruises, broken ribs and heartache. Her ex had shown her the worst side of a Dom-sub relationship. With Luke towering over her, her hands tied in front, her knees shook, but not out of fear. They were liquid with desire, her core tightening, her body screaming for release. Her mind rocked with the realization, her mouth watering for another taste of what was happening to her. How could she be so ready to fall back into that trap?

"You don't have to do anything you don't want to,

Kiki." Jackson's voice cut through the jumbled fog of her thoughts.

"I am my own master," she whispered, her throat dry in anticipation.

"Not in this house." Mark crossed his arms over his chest. "If you don't like it, you can leave." He jerked his head, indicating the exit.

Audrey's gaze skittered toward the door, her breaths now coming in short, rapid succession. She didn't want to go. "No."

Jackson's eyes narrowed. "All you have to do is say the word and I'll kill them."

"I know my limits." Her chin rose. "If I want you to stop, I'll let you know."

Luke crossed his arms, much like Mark. "How?"

"I'll say crackerjack." She laughed, reminded of the little boxes of caramel-coated popcorn. As a child, she'd had so much of the sticky-sweet, candied corn, she'd gotten sick. Could she have too much of a good thing by letting all three of the Gray Wolf brothers touch her? Last time she'd been surrounded by men lusting after her, she'd been stripping for her rent money, unwilling to let her customers touch her. When she'd bought the bar, she'd sworn never to wear the mask, chaps and boots of her alter ego Kiki again.

Never say never.

She didn't need the money and could have canceled had she wanted. Audrey had taken this gig for a no-strings-attached chance to get lucky with

Jackson Gray Wolf. She'd pushed him away after the incident in the storeroom, unwilling to give up her independence or show any signs of weakness. The bar business wasn't for sissies or women, the previous owner had warned her.

Audrey had bought the bar anyway, and set out to prove everyone in the county wrong. Having a fling with a local didn't fall into her plans. Disguised as a stripper, no one need ever know she'd gotten her sex fix with the man of her dreams. No one could prick her Achilles' heel and watch her bleed to death if Jackson pulled the old fuck-'n'-dump so many of the men she knew did. And if she felt like she was losing control, she'd leave and no one would know where to find Kiki.

And to have all three of the Gray Wolf brothers at once was an unexpected bonus. If she had to play by their rules, so be it, as long as her identity remained a secret and she came away satisfied.

"You understand what we might ask of you?" Mark turned her to face him.

She nodded slowly, swallowing hard on her nerves, willing the rapid beat of her heart to slow. "This is some kind of Dom-sub thing, right?" A shiver of excitement skittered across her skin.

Jackson's lips pressed into a thin line. "You're going too far," he warned, his gaze shooting between his brothers.

Audrey shook her head. "No, we aren't. Kiki is willing to try anything." She would have clapped her hands together had they not been bound, ready to take on a little BDSM.

"Do you talk of yourself in third person often?" The big Kiowa Indian's eyes narrowed, and he stared hard at Audrey.

"*I'm* willing to try anything." Audrey fought to keep her cool and not blow her cover, kicking herself for her vocal blunder.

"Trust us, brother. I won't take Kiki anywhere she doesn't want to go." Luke glanced from Jackson to Audrey. "Crackerjack it is." He grinned, then his face smoothed into a confident mask, and he tugged hard on the bindings around her wrists. "Dance for Kiowa warrior Master Gray Wolf."

CHAPTER FOUR

*J*ackson had never been involved in anything quite like what the boys had in mind. And damned if he could stop it from happening. His entire body radiated the heat of a bubbling volcano.

Kiki spun away from him, her chaps flapping wide, her buttocks shining in the light from the strobe. Her hips swirled in a figure-eight motion, with ever-widening thrusts like an experienced belly dancer. She raised her bound hands in the air and turned again to face him. Her black lace bra was thin, sheer, the strategic placement of the thicker lace flower petals covering the tips of her nipples.

Jackson wanted to reach out and yank off the scrap of lace. He yearned to pluck the hidden fruit beneath with his teeth, or tongue the nipples into tight little buds.

How could he make love in a storeroom with one

woman the day before and want to fuck the stuffing out of another in less than twenty-four hours? It wasn't right. Nothing about this night had been right from the start. Yet he couldn't walk away. Didn't want to. He'd made no promises to Audrey. In fact, Audrey had pushed him away, calling their hookup a mistake.

The dancer circled behind him.

Jackson struggled to keep from spinning on his seat, his heart pounding. Instead he glared at his brothers. "You'll pay."

"We already did, brother. We already did." Mark nodded, his smile stretching across his face. "And she's worth every penny."

The blonde hooked her bound hands over his head in a body-rubbing hug, her fingers slipping down over his naked chest. Warm, soft skin nudged his back, the lace bra abrading his skin in a sensuous, side-to-side motion.

Fingers slipped downward, the nails digging into his abdomen, scraping gently upward.

A moan escaped his throat, and he leaned his head back into the cushion of her luscious breasts.

Dear Lord, had he lost all sense of propriety? His brothers were watching as his cock swelled and a strange woman caressed his naked chest.

Jackson's dick twitched, his groin tightening even more. He shifted on the hard wooden seat. Nothing short of shedding his jeans would alleviate the constraints on his manhood.

Luke crossed his arms over his chest, his face stern, his eyes twinkling. "Enough teasing. Show my brother what he can have."

Her hands slid lower, and she ran her fingers across the tip of his cock. Then she was gone, her warmth removed from Jackson's back.

Spinning in his stool, he watched as she shimmied and gyrated around the room, her body languid, graceful and sexy as hell.

Jackson turned in his seat as she came back around to face him. When he started to rise, she laid her hands on his shoulder and pressed him back on the hard wood.

Before he could move, she straddled his lap, her high-heeled, booted feet planted on either side of his thighs, her pussy at mouth level. Nothing stood between Jackson and her cunt but a thin scrap of white material.

His mind fogged with lust, Jackson's hands reached for her hips, grasping her hard, his fingers digging into her bare bottom. He dragged her down until her pussy perched over his jutting member.

"Not so fast, Kiki." Mark grabbed her hand and spun her out of Jackson's grip.

Jackson growled and rose half out of his seat. "Is this my birthday or not?"

Luke, the logical one of the twins, lifted his hands, palms upward, his expression serious, no hint of laughter. "You were the one who didn't want anything. The least you can do is let us have a little fun too."

With a wicked spark in his eyes, Mark nodded. "Kiki, you're making me hot. Too hot for these jeans. Do something about it."

Kiki rubbed her body along Mark's, purring like a cat in heat. Her hand cupped his crotch, squeezing gently.

Anger warred with the rapid rise of desire inside Jackson. How could he be turned on by watching a woman coming on to his own brother? At once jealous and intrigued, he couldn't fathom his own reaction, nor could he glance away. Damn Mark for the rebel he was. He had to be the instigator, coming up with stunts Luke would never dream of. Luke usually kept a level head and made smart choices— except when Mark talked him into some crazy scheme. And this had to be the craziest.

Jackson groaned as Kiki slipped the button loose on Mark's jeans and eased the zipper down. When his cock dipped out, she grasped it, sliding her fingers along the hard length, her gaze not on her hands or even Mark. No, she glanced across at Jackson, a smile teasing the corners of her mouth.

"Suck it," Mark commanded. "Suck my dick."

Was that her body quivering?

Jackson's gaze narrowed, and he watched for her to do it again.

Kiki dropped to her knees, maneuvering herself and Mark sideways so that Jackson could see everything. Her fingers curled around Mark's cock and she bent forward, kissing the tip of his dick, her full, soft lips pressing gently to the rounded head.

Air caught in Jackson's throat and lodged there.

Mark grabbed the back of Kiki's head and pushed her forward, forcing her to take the full length of him into her mouth.

Jackson snarled. "Don't hurt her."

His brother pulled his cock from her mouth. "Am I hurting you?"

"N-no. Not at all." With bound hands, she gripped his dick and drew him back into her mouth.

"Damn, I'm getting horny." Luke flung himself on the floor on his back and lifted one of Kiki's knees, sliding beneath her. "Want some of what you're giving?" he asked.

Kiki let Mark's cock slide free of her mouth, nodding. "Yes."

Pushing the white bikini thong aside, Luke tongued her cunt. "Mmm...I never dreamed of eating a woman in chaps and boots."

Jackson could take it no longer. He stood so fast, the wooden stool crashed to the floor behind him. "Damn it, it's *my* birthday!"

Luke laughed from beneath Kiki's pussy. "Was wondering when he'd wake up."

"Kiki, our brother is feeling neglected." Mark stepped back, freeing her mouth. "Suck his cock hard. He obviously needs it more than I do."

She slid her fingers along Mark's cock and turned

toward Jackson. Color rose high in her cheeks as she climbed to her feet. "Does the birthday boy want it?"

"Damn it!" Jackson pointed down. "Does it look like I want it?"

A chuckle rose from her throat, sending waves of heat radiating from Jackson's chest all the way down into his rock-hard cock.

The dancer's hips rotated left, then right, her arms rising above her head, wrists still bound. As she neared Jackson, her movements became more pronounced, her studded boots scooting across the floor, much like a pair Jackson had seen recently.

A niggle of recognition tugged at Jackson's lust-fogged consciousness.

When Kiki stopped in front of him, her arms dropped, her pale eyes peering through the mask. "What exactly do you want?"

For a long moment, Jackson stared into those eyes, that twinge of something nagging at the back of his mind. "Do I know you?"

Her eyelids drooped low at the same time as her lips curved upward. "If not, you will soon. I am yours to command. Please...command me." Her knees bent, and she kneeled on the floor at his feet.

Jackson stared across at his brothers, not quite sure how to play the game they'd begun. Not even certain he could with a stranger.

Luke nodded at him. "Go ahead. Tell her what you want."

"Are you sure this is what you want?" Jackson

asked her.

She looked up at him, her eyes glowing from the holes in the mask. "Oh, yes."

"In front of my brothers?"

"It excites me." She touched the tip of his exposed cock. "It makes me feel hot." Her hands curled around his dick, and she tugged him closer, until her lips were practically touching his member. "It makes me feel...nasty." The last word came out on a puff of air, warming his cock. She opened her mouth and sucked him into her moist heat.

Jackson's head dropped back, and he moaned.

Slim fingers slid between his thighs, pulling him closer then pushing him away.

"Mind if I join?" Mark knelt behind Kiki, reaching around her to cup her breasts.

"I sure as hell do." Jackson glared at his younger brother.

As usual, his brother ignored his ire and continued caressing the woman's lace-covered breasts. "Hey, big brother, don't you want to see what's hiding behind the bra?" Mark pressed a kiss on Kiki's shoulder.

Hell yes he did, but he wasn't going to tell Mark that.

"You know you do, even if you won't say it." Mark nibbled at Kiki's ear. "Wanna show him?"

AUDREY'S PUSSY creamed at the titillating way Mark

blew warm air over her wet earlobe. "Umm-hmmm," she murmured, her mouth full of Jackson's cock.

"What do you say to the master?" Mark prompted.

Her mouth slid free of Jackson's dick. "Please?" Her chest swelled outward, filling Mark's palms.

"Show him."

She sucked Jackson's cock back into her mouth, her fingers digging into his balls, urging him deep until he bumped against the back of her throat.

"You see, Jack? She wants you to observe what she has to offer." One of Mark's hands circled behind Audrey and flipped the hooks open, releasing her size-C cups of their restraint. The other hand slipped beneath the lace and pinched the nipple hard.

Audrey gasped around the swollen member stretching her lips wide, her teeth scraping against his thickness.

"Careful." Jackson's fingers dug into her hair. "No biting."

She traced a path to the end of his dick before she released him. "Or what?" A streak of rebellion flared and she nipped the tip of his engorged cock.

"Ouch!" Jackson jerked away. "I told you no biting."

Audrey touched a finger to her lips. "Have I been naughty?"

"Oh, yes. You have." Mark slipped the bra down over her arms where it bunched at her bound wrists. "You should teach her who is boss, big brother."

Mark's hands grasped Audrey's hips, lifting her to her feet.

"What are you going to do to me?" All the fantasies she'd had about rough sex pushed forward in her mind, screaming for her to play them out. Her mask hid her identity. No one would know her secret. What could it hurt to get a little enjoyment out of some heavy-handed fucking?

"I don't know. What do you suggest?" Jackson stared at her breasts, his tongue snaking out to wet his lips.

Audrey's nipples puckered at the longing in his eyes. She wanted him to take her breasts into his mouth, to drive his dick into her pussy. To spank her ass until it was bright red and burning.

She turned and bent, presenting her bare bottom to him. "Spank me." Gooseflesh pebbled her skin, and she waited for the pain.

"Really?" Jackson's hands lifted to caress each cheek. "You weren't that bad."

"Oh, yes. I was really bad." She backed closer to him, her ass pushing against his hand. "I deserve to be spanked. Hard."

"Good grief, Jackson. The woman needs a spanking. Either you do it or Luke and I will." Mark winked at her. "Want to suck my cock while my wuss of a brother makes up his mind?"

Audrey reached out and caressed Mark's cock. "Most assuredly tempting."

Jackson dragged her backward. He sat down hard

in the wooden stool, forcing her belly-down over his thighs, his dick pressing into her side. "You really want me to spank you?"

"Yes." She gasped, her breathing labored by excitement. "Spank me hard."

Jackson's hand connected with her bare buttocks, the sound loud, the resulting sting barely noticeable.

"You call that a spanking?" Luke snorted. "I've seen you pat a dog's head harder than that. You didn't even make a red mark."

"I don't want to hurt her." Jackson's hand rested on Audrey's bottom, his thumb hooked into the string parting the cheeks of her ass.

"I deserve the pain. Please, spank me harder." Audrey couldn't believe she was asking for it, practically begging for the pain. After Randy's abuse, she never through she'd want the pain again. Her pussy ached, leaking come at the very thought of Jackson's hand slapping down hard on her skin. "I've been very naughty." She pushed up on her boots, presenting her ass higher.

Jackson popped the string of her thong and shifted beneath her, his cock hard and hot, pressing into her ribs. Her bound hands longed to circle the solid flesh, to run the length of him over and over until he shot his wad all over her naked breasts.

It had been a long time since Audrey allowed her darkest needs to surface. Men would call her strange if they knew of her need for pain, her desire to be dominated and her passion for punishment. She'd played to her inner desires with toys and pinchers, hiding away in her darkened room, never completely satisfied but afraid to give over total control again. But toys weren't enough. She wanted the presence of a man, his cock thick, warm and hard, ready to fill her, to stretch her channel until she screamed out his name in a cataclysmic orgasm.

Her ass hiked higher. She could have all that, here and now, with Jackson Gray Wolf. Hell, she could have Jackson and his brothers if she wanted. If Jackson allowed her to take on more than just his own desires.

With her breasts rubbing against the coarse fabric of his denim jeans, Audrey's anticipation built.

Jackson's hand tapped lightly once, twice, and then left her ass.

Breath caught in Audrey's throat and for a fleeting moment, she knew it was over. Jackson would never hurt a female. Good guys never did. And Jackson was a top-notch good guy. A cowboy in a white hat.

Then his hand landed hard against her ass, the sting so sharp it brought ready tears to her eyes.

"Oh, yes!" she cried before she could think clearly.

"Like that?"

"Yes!" Audrey squirmed against his thighs, her ass rising, a target he couldn't possibly miss. "I've been bad. Oh so bad."

"Who is your master?" Jackson demanded.

"You are my master," she replied promptly,

wanting him to smack her again, her core tightening to a fever pitch.

"What of my brothers?"

Audrey hesitated, unsure of what he wanted to hear. "In your absence, they are my masters?"

"Wrong." He slapped her bottom.

Audrey whimpered, on the verge of an orgasm so massive she could barely breathe.

"I am your only master. If you want my brothers, you have to ask my permission."

"And if I don't?" Her body quivered, her ears perking, anxious to hear the punishment for any infraction.

"I will tie you to my bed and torture you."

Her pussy squeezed tight, the juices running out, drenching her thong panties. "How will you torture me? Please, tell me."

"I will bring you to the edge of orgasm and stop." His hand smoothed over the spot that stung on her bottom, the gentle movement more painful than if he'd slapped her again.

Audrey moaned.

"Do you want my brothers?"

She nodded.

Jackson slapped her ass. "Do you want my brothers?"

"No." She moaned again, reduced to a quivering mass of hyper-sensitive nerve endings begging for release only Jackson could give. "I want you to fuck me. Only you."

"That's better." He lifted her and positioned her legs to straddle him on the stool.

When she would have eased down over his cock, he held her up and away, his fingers digging into her hips. "But not yet. You will come when I tell you that you can. Not any sooner."

Audrey's thighs clenched around his, her legs shaking with her need for him to be inside her. "When?"

"As soon as I can get a condom."

Mark and Luke laughed out loud and scrambled out of the room. They were back in seconds, each carrying a long strip of condoms. They slapped them in Jackson's hands and stood back, grins stretching from ear to ear.

Audrey didn't care if Mark and Luke watched. All of her focus remained on Jackson and the cock only inches from her heated core.

But Jackson glared at his brothers. "The show's over."

The twins' faces fell.

Mark spoke first. "Oh, come on."

Luke jabbed his brother in the ribs. "You heard the guy, let's leave."

Rubbing his ribs, his lips pressing together in a straight line, Mark sighed. "Fine. But next time I'm hiring her for me alone."

"Like hell." Jackson's gaze never left Audrey. "And never mind leaving."

Mark's frown brightened into a smile. "You mean you'll share?"

Audrey almost laughed at Mark's comical expression, except that all their talk delayed her ultimate satisfaction. "If you three are going to talk, *I'll* just leave."

"Like hell." Jackson stood, lifting Audrey up and off him.

Disappointment shot through her. She hadn't expected her comment to bring their game to a halt.

Then she was thrown up and over Jackson's shoulder in a fireman's carry, the force of her gut landing on his shoulder, knocking all the air from her lungs.

"You two can stay out here. Kiki is coming with me." Jackson strode from the living room, the strobe light fading to dark as he carried her down the unlit hallway to the master suite.

Audrey didn't speak until they entered the room where only a sliver of moonlight shone through the blinds. "What if I don't want to do it with you now?"

"You only have to say your word and I'll stop." He flipped her over his shoulder, landing her on the bed.

She stared up at the cowboy, her heart hammering, scared for the first time since this little charade began. Would she be able to stop him once he started? Would he hurt her like she'd been hurt before?

Jackson straightened and ripped his jeans down his legs, stepping out of them. In the soft glow of moonlight, his body glistened a silvery blue, broad shoulders filling the room.

Her breathing coming in ragged gulps, Audrey lost her confidence. What if he found out who she was? Would that change the way he thought about her? Would he be disappointed to discover Audrey Anderson, the owner of the Ugly Stick, had some sick fantasies lurking inside?

She opened her mouth to say crackerjack, but didn't get the first consonant out before Jackson flipped her onto her belly.

"Get on your knees," he demanded.

"What are you going to do?"

"I'm going to fuck you hard."

All thoughts of calling the party off fled Audrey's mind. "And if I don't get up on my knees?" she dared to ask, knowing she would garner some kind of punishment, her pulse racing in anticipation.

"Do it, or I'll make you do it."

Her stubborn streak refused to let her back down, the excitement of his next moves making Audrey dare to be rebellious. "No."

Jackson grabbed her hair and pulled.

Audrey yelped and came up on her knees, afraid the pins holding the wig in place would come loose and expose her for the fraud she was.

"That's more like it." Jackson climbed up on the bed behind her and nudged her with the tip of his cock. "Want it?"

"No." She wanted the pain with the fucking.

With her back to him, she didn't know what he'd do next, couldn't read his expression.

The sharp slap on her ass made her jump, the stinging sensation heightening her lust, filling her pussy with come.

"You will not come until I give you permission."

"Who said I was coming?" Her words came out on an unconvincing gasp.

"I can see how wet and ready you are." His finger traced her opening, swirling in the juices her body produced at the mere sound of his voice.

Dear Lord, the man had more power over her than he could ever imagine.

To Audrey that was as frightening as it was exhilarating.

Jackson licked a path to her opening, replacing the smooth strokes of his hands, tonguing her cunt, finger-fucking her from behind. His thumb dipped into her juices and traced a line up to the tight round ring of her anus. He poked it in, sliding in and out while his tongue laved her clit and pussy.

Tension mounted, the tingling sensation beginning at her core spreading throughout her body. "I'm going to come. I can't stop it."

"No, not until I say you can."

Her hands clasped together in the bindings, Audrey cried, "I can't stop it."

"You can and will." Jackson backed away, and a cool waft of air-conditioned air brushed across Audrey's pussy, doing little to chill the heat inside.

"Please," she whispered. "Please don't stop now."

Rough hands clasped her hips and a thick, hot rod slammed into her channel, filling, stretching and sliding in and out.

He leaned down over her, his breath warm on the back of her neck. "What is your real name, woman? Who are you?"

She shuddered, biting hard on her lip to keep from screaming out. Instead she gasped, "Kiki."

"I don't believe you."

"It's all you'll get."

He slapped her ass harder, the sting making Audrey's heart beat faster, her pussy clenching around his shaft. She wanted more. "My name is Kiki!" she shouted defiantly, knowing the consequences and welcoming the forthcoming punishment as he spanked her again.

The tingling sensations and having Jackson inside her like this was more exquisite than Audrey could have imagined. She shot up and over in seconds, her body jerking with each spasm of her orgasm.

"I told you not to come until I gave you permission." Jackson slapped her ass, the resounding noise echoing off the walls of the room. He slapped her again and slammed his cock deep inside her, the force of his thrust carrying her forward until her head bumped the headboard.

Audrey braced her bound hands against the wood, reveling in his rough treatment, rocking back into his next plunge deep inside her. She wanted all of him, hard, fast and forceful. The second wave of an earth-shattering orgasm swept over her. When she came, Jackson thrust one last time, burying his dick to the hilt, his hands holding her bottom tightly against his groin, his body stiff. Only his cock moved, twitching and jerking, surrounded by her channel, pumping his seed into the ribbed condom.

When he finally collapsed, taking her down beside him on the bed, Audrey lay still, her eyes closed, her body shaking with the intensity of what they'd just experienced.

"Are you all right?" he whispered.

"More than all right." She chuckled softly. "I'm satisfied."

Her mask shifted, rising up over her cheekbone. She hadn't realized she still wore her chaps. Her thong panties had been shredded somewhere between the living room and the bedroom, and hell if she knew where her bra had landed.

She couldn't have moved if she wanted to.

With Jackson's arms pulling her against him, spooning her body into his big, muscular frame, Audrey didn't want to consider tomorrow. It would come soon enough. Then she'd have to think of some way to keep her secret. One thing was certain, making love with Jackson the way they had tonight and for the second time in as many days had changed everything.

She wasn't sure she was ready for the repercussions.

CHAPTER FIVE

*L*ater in the night, Jackson woke with a rock-hard boner and stared up into pale blue eyes. They peered at him through a swath of a black mask, their pale irises reflecting the moonlight.

Kiki straddled him, still wearing the chaps and nothing else, her bra somewhere in the other room, her boots lying on the floor where she'd kicked them off after their first wild and raunchy round of fucking.

His cock filled her, pressing deep inside her heated, slick warmth.

She rose on her haunches, cool air licking at the base of his balls. Then she lowered over him ever so slowly, her channel tightening around him, gripping him like a snug, juicy glove.

Her pace increased until she practically bounced over him, ratcheting up and down like a piston.

Jackson grabbed her waist, flipped her over on

her back and slid a pillow beneath her hips. Then he knelt between her thighs, draping her long, smooth legs over his shoulders.

"Ready for this?" he asked.

"Don't make me wait."

"Is that a demand?"

"No, a request." She closed her eyes and inhaled deeply. "Please."

Leaning over her, he stared down at her, his chin tipped upward. "Who is your master?"

"You are."

"Then tell me what you want." He paused.

Her hands, still bound at the wrists, slipped over her stomach and down to the furry mound, parting her folds. "I want you to eat me."

"How bad?"

"So bad, I'd do anything for you."

"I'll take that as a promise." He leaned forward and ran his tongue across her pussy and up through her folds to tap the tip of her clit. "Like that?" he said, his mouth leaving her sweetness.

"Oh, yessss." She writhed beneath him, her hips rising to find his mouth.

He licked her, this time pausing to suck her nubbin between his teeth. He bit down gently.

Her back arched, pushing her bottom up off the pillow. "Oh, yes."

"Does that hurt?" he asked.

"Yes. Oh, yes!" she cried, her bound hands curling

into his hair and bringing him back to her. "More, please."

Jackson obliged, biting down again then licking to ease the pain. Her body settled into a steady rocking motion, matching his tongue's thrusts against her clit. He swept low and surged into her channel, swirling in the musky, salty juices, his cock twitching, ready to fill her.

He pushed her thighs open wide, then climbed up her body and drove into her until his balls slapped her ass.

Kiki's legs wrapped around his waist, clinging to him, drawing him ever closer, her muscles tightening and loosening with every stroke.

Tension intensified in his groin, tingling sensations shooting out to every nerve as he catapulted over the edge into a fiery abyss. His thrusts continued until he could move no more. With one hand, he pulled the pillow from beneath Kiki's hips and wrapped the other arm around her, rolling to the side, maintaining their intimate connection.

Exhausted and fulfilled, Jackson drifted to sleep, his hand cupping one of her breasts, feeling more replete than he'd felt in a very long time. As his thoughts faded into darkness, he reminded himself to find out who Kiki really was. He had to see her again.

AS SOON AS his eyes closed, it seemed light pushed past the slits of Jackson's eyelids, forcing its way into his vision. Surely it wasn't morning already. He didn't want to get up, not when he had a soft, willing woman in the bed beside—

Jackson sat up straight and peered at the empty pillow which still sported a slight indentation from Kiki's head. He tossed the sheets aside and leaped to his feet, racing into the master bath.

Empty.

Back in the bedroom, he pulled on his jeans, buttoning them while his gaze panned the master bedroom. Surely she hadn't gone without saying anything? Maybe she'd left a note.

Anger spurred his actions as he flung the pillows aside and dropped to his knees to see if perhaps the note had slid to the floor. No woman could be that good in bed and not mean it, not have any kind of emotional connection. She couldn't have disappeared without saying some-thing, anything.

Beneath a tumble of blankets and the comforter he found a single bright red boot. So that was the true color of the dark boots Kiki had worn the night before.

Jackson jumped to his feet, his heart hammering, his fingers running across the red leather and bright metal studs, lovingly polished and cared for.

In the light of day, un-befuddled by black lights, strobes and a sexy dancer, the significance of the red boot hit him square between the eyes.

He knew that boot. Hell, he knew the only

woman who wore kickass red boots anywhere in the tri-county region.

A grin spread across his face, all anger seeping away as he realized just who the illusive stripper was. Kiki might be her name while wearing a mask, but Jackson knew, beneath the wig, boots and chaps, she was the owner of the Ugly Stick Saloon, Audrey Anderson.

He dragged on his own boots and ran out of the room, the door slamming wide open as he hurried through the house.

"Going somewhere?" Mark stepped in front of him before he could reach the door.

A growl rose up Jackson's throat, and he fought to keep from shoving his brother out of the way. "I'm going to town."

"We have a truck coming today to haul the cattle to auction. Did your birthday present make you forget?" Mark's brows rose as his arms crossed over his chest. "By the way, Luke and I decided we'd hire Kiki again. She's quite the stripper. Possibly a little more than one man can handle."

Jackson's jaw tightened. "She's not for sale."

Luke stepped up beside Mark. "Didn't say she was. Just that she's for hire as a stripper. She must have liked you enough to go further than we contracted."

"Shut up." Jackson shoved Mark aside and pushed through the front screen door.

"We'll need help getting the cattle culled and

herded into the pen. You gonna be here?" Mark called out as he and Luke followed Jackson outside.

Jackson stopped halfway down the front porch steps, torn between what he had to do and what he wanted to do. He wanted to do Kiki—or her alter ego —again...now. But with the cattle truck en route and not a minute to spare to get the steers separated from the rest of the herd, he'd need to be there alongside his brothers.

Damn.

"I'll be there."

Luke glanced at the sky. "Sun's gonna be brutal today." He grinned. "You might want to wear a shirt." Then he sauntered past Jackson and headed for the barn.

Mark followed Luke, both chuckling as if sharing a joke.

The joke was on Jackson. Why should he be all wound up about a woman? A lying woman, who'd made love to him in disguise rather than be on the up-and-up as herself. What was she afraid of?

Jackson sighed. The answers to his questions would have to wait until they loaded the cattle going to auction. He tromped back up the stairs and into the house for that shirt he'd need, cursing life as a cattle rancher for the first time since he'd taken over. Solving the mystery of Kiki would have to wait.

Damn.

For the next ten hours, he and his brothers wrangled cattle, herding, cutting and loading them into the trailers that would carry them to auction. When the last steer trundled up the ramp, Jackson, Mark and Luke dragged their dusty, dirty and tired bodies back to the house for a shower and a cold dinner.

The clock struck ten by the time Jackson climbed out of the shower. Longer summer days only meant more time to work, meaning less time to play. And even less time to follow a woman to the Ugly Stick Saloon.

His body ached—he'd been kicked enough times he'd have bruises to show for weeks—but his livelihood was loaded onto a truck, and soon he'd have enough money to pay the mortgage for the next few months.

He sighed, happy to have one major accomplishment under his belt. But he sure as hell didn't have the energy to pursue the owner of the red boot. Not tonight.

Not until the next night did he get over to the Ugly Stick Saloon to follow up on a full-blown hunch and a red boot. The additional time had given him perspective and time to hatch a plan.

THE DOOR to the storeroom banged open. "Where do you want this whisky?"

Audrey teetered on the stepladder and almost fell. "Charli! Don't scare me like that!"

Charli set the box of whisky on a shelf and held out her hand. "Get down before you kill yourself."

"I'm fine. I'm almost done cleaning the fifteen-year-old, sticky, spilled wine off this shelf."

"Get down. I'll finish." Charli grabbed Audrey's hand and tugged gently. "You're making me nervous. Hell, you're making all of us nervous."

"What do you mean?" Audrey's cheeks burned as she allowed Charli to pull her down the stepladder to the floor of the storeroom. The storeroom where she and Jackson had first done it. Oh, dear Lord, she hadn't been able to get the man out of her mind for even a minute.

"You're as twitchy as a cat in a room full of rocking chairs," Charli exclaimed.

Twitchy described the way Audrey felt perfectly. Every nerve and blood vessel pounded, keeping her hopping, her body unable to slow down. It was as though she were high on speed with no way to come down.

No, she knew one way, and it wasn't by cleaning fifteen-year-old wine off a storeroom shelf. A tumble in a certain cowboy's bed would set her right. She just wasn't ready to admit she needed a man as much as she needed Jackson Gray Wolf.

"What's bothering you?" Charli asked.

The door to the storeroom opened again, the music from the dancehall spilling through, providing enough noise Audrey wasn't required to answer immediately.

Cory leaned in the doorway. He wore his costume for Ladies' Night Out. Leather vest and chaps over a black thong completed the ensemble. With his white-blond hair and broad shoulders, he'd bring in a ton of money as the women frothed and drank their way into a frenzy. "The show's about to start. Did you want to introduce the dancers?"

For a long moment, Audrey stared at the chaps, her heart slipping through several beats before it resumed a steady thundering pace. Her pussy creamed as she envisioned what she'd done with Jackson in a pair of chaps just like those. "No, no. Let Kendall introduce the dancers. She knows all of you by name."

Cory glanced from Audrey to Charli and back again.

Audrey had always insisted on introducing the dancers on Ladies' Night Out. So? She could step outside the box just once. "Why are you two staring at me? Get to work!" she snapped.

Charli nodded at Cory. "Get Kendall to do it."

As soon as the door shut, Charli grabbed Audrey's arms and pushed her against the nearest shelf. "What's wrong? Why are you acting so weird?"

Audrey struggled between yelling at her assistant and bursting into tears. Last night, she'd come to work, fully expecting Jackson Gray Wolf to blow through the doors, demanding to see Kiki.

He hadn't.

She ducked her head and tried to wiggle her way out of Charli's grip. "Nothing's wrong. Just let me do my job."

"Not until you tell me what happened the other night at the Gray Wolf party." Charli stared hard into her eyes. "You danced for them, didn't you?"

"I told you, Audrey Anderson doesn't dance for anyone anymore." She flung back her shoulders, tipping her head high.

"Okay, so Audrey Anderson doesn't dance for anyone anymore." Charli's mouth twisted into a wry grin. "You didn't really answer my question."

"Leave it, Charli."

"No." Charli didn't budge, her lips set in a firm line.

"Leave it, or I'll fire you."

Charli shook her head. "You can't fire me. I'm the only one you trust to leave the bar to when you want to take a day off."

"I can get Kendall to take over."

"She's too busy with her man to pay close-enough attention to the way things run here."

"She'd do fine." Audrey pushed away from Charli and grabbed a bottle of wine, heading for the stepladder.

Charli stepped in her way. "You're avoiding the issue. What happened? Did you and Jackson hook up?"

"Damn it, Charli, it's none of your business. But if you must know, Jackson and Audrey Anderson did not hook up."

A frown creased Charli's brow. "Wow, you're freakin' me out. That's the second time tonight you've talked about yourself in the third person. You are usually with it and completely together. I've never seen you so...so...unhinged."

"I'm not unhinged." She shook the bottle of wine at Charli. "I'm Audrey, the same boss you've had for two years. Nothing's changed, I tell you. Nothing!" The bottle slipped from her grasp and crashed to the floor, splattering dark red wine over Charli's jean-clad legs and Audrey's white boots.

Charli stared down at the mess, her gaze focusing not on the wine but on the boots.

Audrey groaned inwardly, bracing herself.

"You're wearing white boots." Charli's head came up and she stared at Audrey. "What happened to your red boots?"

With a shrug, Audrey squatted, fishing through the sticky wine for the broken shards of glass. "I didn't feel like wearing them. Now will you help me clean up this mess or get out of my way so that I can do it by myself?"

Charli dropped to her haunches in front of Audrey and grabbed her wrist, plucking the glass from her hands one piece at a time. "Honey, you know you can tell me anything."

Tears welled in Audrey's eyes and she blinked rapidly, wishing them away. "There's nothing to tell," she said, her voice choking on the words. And she wasn't lying. As far as Audrey was concerned, there was nothing to tell. Now Kiki, on the other hand, had a huge story to tell. But Kiki wasn't coming out to play ever again.

A sob rose in Audrey's throat, and she looked down before Charli could see the tears in her eyes.

Charli sighed, then spoke quietly. "Maybe you should take the night off or something. The place runs itself on Ladies' Night Out. Why don't you go take a drive down to the lake or go home and soak in a bubble bath."

Audrey opened her mouth to protest and closed it before uttering a word. Charli was right. She was no good to anyone the way she was tonight. A soak in the tub would do her body good. Maybe then she could shake Jackson Gray Wolf out of her thoughts.

Yeah, right.

She handed over the loose shards of glass and left the storeroom. She couldn't get out of the bar fast enough, avoiding talking to anyone who dared to get in her way.

Her cell phone rang in her hip pocket, and she pulled it out, answering before she thought better.

"Audrey, it's Luke Gray Wolf. Any chance of getting Kiki back here tonight?"

Audrey's feet ground to a halt. "No, that's impossible. She's not for hire."

"Well, damn. She made quite an impression the other night, not only on me and Mark but on Jackson as well. If we don't do something soon, he's liable to blow a gasket on us."

"Sorry, boys. She's not interested." Her voice faltered.

"You sure? We'll pay her double what we paid before. We really need her in a bad way."

Audrey's heart skipped several beats, her determination wavering. What Luke and Mark had done to her two nights ago to get her lathered up for Jackson was very near to orgasmic.

"If you think she'll reconsider, would you give her our number?" Luke persisted.

"I'll think about it." Audrey pressed the off button.

As she left the building, Audrey swerved into the prop room and grabbed a spare set of stripper's chaps. Rolling the leather into a tight wad, she stuffed it into the oversized purse she carried her files and laptop in. Why she did it, she couldn't say. Maybe Kiki had a mind of her own.

A shiver of excitement slipped over her skin, speeding her footsteps until she was running for her truck. When she shifted into drive, she didn't head to Temptation and home, she turned in the opposite direction, making a beeline for the Gray Wolf Ranch and three hot cowboys. She hoped like hell that the natives were restless tonight, because she sure as hell was.

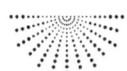

CHAPTER SIX

*J*ackson pulled into the parking lot of the Ugly Stick Saloon, dismayed at the number of cars, trucks and SUVs lined up on the gravel and spilling into the grass. What the hell was going on tonight? A line of women stood at the door waiting to get in. The marquis read *Ladies' Night Out.*

With a groan, Jackson drove around the back of the saloon and double-parked. Hopefully he'd get in and back out without any trouble.

A large woman dressed in jeans and cowboy boots, her hair cut short, almost butch, fingers pinching the butt of a burned-out cigarette, stood at the rear entrance.

"Unless you're the talent, you ain't gettin' in." She flicked the butt into the gravel at his feet and crossed ham-hock arms over her chest.

"Hi, Greta Sue, I need to see Audrey." Jackson

stepped to the side, intent on going around the woman.

She cut him off, moving her bulk with surprising speed. "I said, if you ain't the talent, you ain't gettin' in." She placed a fat hand on his chest and pushed him.

Other than hitting the woman, Jackson had no recourse but to back down. "Can you at least go get Audrey and tell her Jackson is here and would like to talk to her?"

The woman shook her head. "No can do."

"Why?"

The woman's face cracked into a grin. "She ain't here."

Jackson sucked in a deep breath and let it out slowly. "Why didn't you say so in the first place?"

"You didn't ask if the boss was here."

"But—" Jackson stared into the woman's squinty eyes and shrugged. "Guess you got a point." He turned to leave.

"You coulda got in by saying you were the talent, you know."

Jackson glanced over his shoulder at Greta Sue, whose grin had spread across her face, making her less intimidating and more jovial.

Her gaze raked him from head to toe. "Ya got the build for it. Wouldn't mind seein' ya in a G-string myself."

Jackson tipped his cowboy hat. "Mighty kind of

you. But I think I'll keep my pants on." He winked and walked away.

"Cryin' shame," she muttered behind him.

Jackson climbed into his pickup and pulled away from the Ugly Stick. As he drove toward home, his left foot tapped the floorboard. Maybe he should visit Audrey at her home.

Nah. She might not even be there. Why drive all the way over to Temptation just to find an empty house? That brand of reasoning led to another thought. What if Audrey was out on a date, or worse, out dancing for another man?

His hands tightening on the steering wheel, Jackson gritted his teeth. The woman had pushed him away, stating their storeroom fuck was a mistake. If that was true, then why the hell did she show up as Kiki at his house and spend the night mattress-wrangling with him?

She wasn't making sense. Well not to a man anyway. Possibly she was doin' some of that female thinkin'. Either way, he had a boot to prove Audrey and Kiki were one and the same. What he didn't know was why Audrey felt she had to disguise herself as Kiki to feel comfortable making love to him again. Or maybe it was the rough-riding, kinky sex she didn't like to admit to lovin'.

Jackson had a plan on how to bring Audrey around to revealing herself, but he needed to find Audrey to set the plan in motion. He pounded the steering wheel with his palm, frustrated at having to wait.

As he pulled into the yard at the ranch, he stared at the darkened living room windows. Had the boys gone to bed early for once? It wasn't poker night, the Ugly Stick was off limits to guys and they hadn't said anything about going out that evening.

A bright light blinked in the darkness of the living room.

Jackson's heart skipped a beat.

The light blinked again, then settled into a steady rhythm, strobing the darkness with brilliant flashes.

His stomach flipping over, Jackson jumped down from his truck and ran for the house.

No way. It couldn't be.

As he burst through the front door, a familiar figure swayed in the intermittent lighting, her body smooth, sensual and practically naked, wearing nothing but a thong, a white lace bra and those damned chaps. Instead of the red boots, she wore a pair of white cowboy boots. The long blonde hair scraped the top of her ass, a white cowboy hat balanced on her head at a jaunty angle.

Hallelujah! Jackson's heart sang. She'd come back.

Heat surged beneath his collar. She'd come back to dance for his brothers, not him.

Mark sat in the wooden stool Jackson had occupied the night before, a grin splitting his face, his hands reaching for the woman cavorting in front of him.

Luke glanced toward Jackson. "Told you she'd come back. All I had to do was call the Ugly Stick and here she is." Luke stood with his shirt off, his jeans riding low on his hips, his feet bare on the wooden floor.

Jackson moved closer, not entirely sure he liked the idea of Kiki dancing for all three of them. After their night in bed, he kinda felt he owned the right to claim her as his.

The anger built until another thought followed on that. Maybe that was Audrey's point to pushing him away and disguising herself as another person. She didn't want to commit to one man. Didn't want anyone staking a claim on her.

That set him back a step or two. What had caused Audrey to be so gun-shy on commitment? Had some fool cheated on her? Maybe Jackson made her feel less than a woman or worse, he hadn't measured up to her sexual appetites.

Jackson edged closer. There had to be a reason.

Kiki spun away from Mark and circled Luke, her hands trailing over his chest, fingers dancing along the man's muscles.

Jackson could almost feel the strength in those hands, the same hands that had wrapped around his cock, guiding him into her mouth. His jeans tightened, his dick pressing against the hard metal rivets.

Luke grabbed Kiki beneath the legs and swung her up in his arms. "You're just about the purdiest thing I've seen." He kissed her soundly and spun her in a circle.

"Hey, don't be greedy. She was dancing for me," Mark complained.

Luke set her on her booted feet, and Kiki danced toward Mark, planting her heels on either side of his thighs, grinding her pelvis toward his face.

Mark clamped his hands on her hips and held them steady as he ran his tongue from her belly-button to the low cut of her thong.

She hooked her thumb in the elastic of the thong and dragged it lower, exposing the furry mound of hair beneath.

Mark plunged his face into it, his fingers clasping the globes of her buttocks.

She laughed and pushed his face away. "That tick-les." Then she turned and sat in his lap, bending to touch her boots.

It gave Mark and Jackson a prime view of her pearly white ass.

Jackson groaned, wanting to join her dance but not yet willing to share with his brothers. Which gave the twins free rein with the beauty. Well, to hell with that.

He stomped into the middle of the room and jerked Kiki by the hand up into his arms, slamming her against his chest.

Her eyes widened and her mouth rounded into a surprised O. Then her eyelids drooped over her blue eyes, the mask still firmly in place.

Jackson reached up to lift the mask.

"Don't, or I leave," she warned, her body shifting against him, her breasts rubbing into his shirt. "You don't want me to leave, do you?"

He shook his head. "No."

"The last time I was here it was your birthday. Tonight it isn't." She ran her fingers up the front of his shirt, over his chin and to his lips.

He captured one and sucked it into his mouth.

"I owe it to your brothers to entertain them tonight. After all, I'm here on their dime." She pulled her finger out of his mouth and pressed her lips to his. "If I don't do a good job, you can spank me." She shrugged and flipped her hair over her shoulders. "If I do a good job, you can spank me. Or not." With a quick spin, she danced out of his arms, her bare bottom, a tempting target, shaking in his face.

How he wanted to bend her over his knee and spank her for teasing him. Then he wanted to drive his cock into her and spank her more.

Jackson stood at the edge of the makeshift dance floor, his arms crossed, his fists clenched.

Kiki spun and swayed around Luke, pressing her bare ass against his. Then she rounded to the front, wrapped her arms around Luke and leaned her breasts into his naked chest. She straddled his thigh, dragging her pussy along the hardened length. "Want to play with my boobs?" she whispered, the sound carrying just enough that Jackson could hear.

Luke nodded. "Hell, yeah!" He reached behind her

and flipped the hooks loose, then slipped the straps over her shoulders and down her arms. He tossed the bra to the side. It landed on top of a lamp and dangled saucily.

Luke's hands rose to cup her breasts, lifting and squeezing them gently.

"Oh, come on, I know you can squeeze harder than that. You're a man, aren't you?" She clamped her hands over his, squeezing firmly.

Jackson didn't think he could get any harder. He jerked the top rivet of his jeans open, releasing some of the pressure. Not nearly enough, but he didn't say a word. He wanted his shot at spanking her when she'd finished teasing his brothers and him in the process.

"Oh, hell, he's not nearly enough man for you. Let me." Mark moved up behind Kiki, shoved Luke's and Kiki's hands off her breasts and pinched the tips between his thumbs and forefingers.

"Mmm, that's nice." Kiki wiggled her bottom into the jutting ridge of Mark's fly, while her hands dropped to Luke's waistband. Her fingers flicked the top button loose. "Wanna come out to play?"

Jackson groaned and turned away. He couldn't take more of this. He just couldn't.

"Oh, hell yeah," Luke whooped loudly.

Like a moth mesmerized by the flame, Jackson couldn't remain with his back to the goings-on in the room. He spun.

Luke had his fly open and his cock jutting into Kiki's hand.

She bent at the waist, Mark leaning over her from behind, his hands still cupping her breasts.

Kiki studied Luke's dick and stretched out her tongue, licking it from the base to the tip. Her pretty pink tongue circled the hole and dipped in. She glanced over her shoulder at Mark. "Aren't you getting hot yet?"

"Who me?" Mark squeaked. "Uh, yeah." He nudged her with his fully clothed groin.

"What are you going to do about it?" She wiggled her bottom again, rubbing against the ridge.

Mark fumbled with the button and zipper, ripping open his fly. His cock sprang free, eliciting another groan from Jackson.

"Why are you doing this to me?" Jackson asked.

Kiki looked up, her brows rising into the bangs of that danged blonde wig. "Doing what?"

"Making me suffer." How he wanted to rip off the wig and expose her long, strawberry-blonde tresses.

"Am I making you suffer? You don't have to watch, you know. Your brothers have everything in hand."

Mark reached into his back pocket and pulled a condom out. He held it up for his brother's inspection. "See. I came prepared." He ripped it open with his teeth and sheathed his shaft in record time.

Jackson stood rooted to the spot, unable to move,

unable to look away as Mark tugged her thong aside and eased his dick into Kiki.

His cock pressed so hard against his fly, Jackson couldn't stand it. He tugged the buttons on his jeans loose in one hard jerk. His member sprang free, giving him immediate, if not short-lived, relief.

Before him, Mark pumped in and out of Kiki as she sucked Luke's cock into her mouth to the same rhythm. Every once in a while, she cast a glance his way as if measuring his reaction to the orgy in front of him.

He was reacting all right. His hand ran the length of his member, sliding over the steely hardness, his concentration flicking from where Mark entered her from one end to Luke from the other. The strobe light blinked, adding to the frenetic intensity of the scene.

Luke grabbed Kiki's head and jerked free of her mouth, his come shooting over the hardwood floor.

Mark held on to her hips, his head thrown back, his body stiffening. He grunted loud and slammed hard into her one last time, holding her steady, his hands sliding along her sides to her breasts, easing her into more of an upright position, his cock still buried deep inside her.

Jackson's hand ratcheted up and down over his dick. The tension had built to match that of his brothers. When he pitched over the edge, he came, his juices squirting out over the floor, drenching his hand.

Luke chuckled. "Big brother got something out of that." He cupped a hand around Kiki's chin and kissed her lips. "That was great. Thanks."

Mark patted her ass and pulled free. "It sure was. Can't remember better." He stretched and yawned. "Well, I'm all done for. I'll call it a night."

"I'm not." Luke stared down at his boner. "I could go another round if you're up to it." He glanced up hopefully at Kiki.

Kiki shot a look at Jackson. "Only if your big brother joins us this time."

Jackson frowned, the evidence of his own ejaculation still gleaming in his hands. Though he'd gotten off by himself, he hadn't gotten the satisfaction of being inside Kiki or playing rough with her as they had two nights before.

"If it's to be Luke and me, I'm calling the shots."

Kiki shrugged, a grin pulling at her lips. "Are you the master?"

Jackson's eyes narrowed and he stalked across the floor, his boots hitting the wood hard. He yanked her into his arms, forcing her chin up so that she had to stare into his eyes. "*You* tell *me*."

Her gaze held his for a long moment, then her eyelids dropped over her blue eyes. "You are the master."

"Hot damn!" Luke clapped his hands together.

Mark hovered near the doorway to the living room. "Can a man change his mind?"

"Hell no—" Jackson started.

Kiki raised her finger to his lips. "Yes, he can."

"Four's a crowd."

Kiki's chin dipped low, a slight smile lifting her lips. "You're the master. As you said, you can call the shots. Remember, I like it rough, but it's my decision who I want to be with, and if I want more than just one man."

Jackson's cock jerked. "What if I want a one-woman man?"

She pulled free of his arms. "Find someone else." She started to walk away.

Unable to let her go, Jackson grabbed her arm and yanked her back against him, his hands rising to cup her breasts. He pinched the nipples hard, rolling them between his thumbs and forefingers. "You'd walk away?" His dick nudged the crease of her ass, pressing toward her anus.

Her breath caught and she paused before whispering, "In a heartbeat."

"So be it. I'll share you with my brothers, but we play by my rules."

Her hands reached behind her, skimming down his waist to his hips. She dragged him closer, his damp cock sliding between her cheeks. "As you wish."

AUDREY DIDN'T KNOW what had gotten into her. From swearing never to fuck Jackson Gray Wolf again to being at his mercy all in the space of forty-eight hours. She knew she had control if she wanted it. But she didn't. Her toys couldn't begin to satisfy her like the Kiowa warrior. And the added bonus of his two brothers was ice cream with the cake.

The question nagging her was how long she could keep up the pretense. Audrey kept telling herself she was only in this charade for the sex. One glance at the tall, dark Texan and she knew it was a lie. She wanted a hell of a lot more out of him than that. But what?

After her relationship with Randy McNabb, the two-timing, abusive son of a bitch she'd hooked up with in Austin, she never wanted a man to dominate her so completely that she didn't know who she was. With Randy she'd lost herself, lost all of her confidence and had been forced to move from Austin to Temptation, Texas to get out from under his heavy hand.

With Jackson, it was different. She'd invited Jackson to dominate her on her own terms. With him, she welcomed the pain. With Randy, she'd come to hate it and flinched away from him. He hadn't understood limits. Jackson did. The two were as different as night and day. That Jackson was willing to share her showed how much he cared about her feelings.

Still, was she ready to reveal herself as Audrey instead of Kiki? She liked when he took control in the bedroom, but she wanted control of her own life in public.

Did she want someone in her life who had such a

sway over her emotions and actions? She'd worked too damned hard to rebuild her shattered life. She had too much riding on the respect she'd earned in this little corner of Texas to lose it now.

No, she couldn't let Jackson in. The mask remained. The relationship would end if the Gray Wolfs ever discovered the truth.

In the meantime, she wanted to lie with the wolves and enjoy a little nooky. Tomorrow Kiki would hang up her boots and chaps and totally disappear from the face of the earth.

CHAPTER SEVEN

*J*ackson pointed to Luke. "Move the table."

Luke snapped to attention and practically leaped at the big coffee table in the middle of the living room floor. Mark hurried to the other side, and together they shoved the table to the corner of the room.

The music played on, the strobe light flickering to the beat. Kiki smiled and pulled away from Jackson, her body writhing, swaying and turning in rhythm to the sexy song playing on the sound system. "What do you want first?" She shimmied, her breasts shaking, bobbing and tempting Jackson into a permanent hard-on.

"On your knees," he demanded.

She danced to the center of the large area rug in the middle of the living room where she dropped to a kneeling position, swaying backward, her hips churning, her arms floating in the air.

God, she was beautiful. Her skin glowed a blue gold, her bleached-blonde wig shifting jerkily in the intermittent light.

Jackson didn't want to think about how he'd include his brothers in this orgy. He just wanted to jump right in and screw Kiki—er, Audrey. But she wanted more than that. If he was to win her trust, he had to go along with her demands, while making a few of his own. This delicate game of Dominance and submission would take a certain amount of finesse if he didn't want to scare her away for good.

Jackson dropped to his knees in front of her, his hands circling her hips, rising to capture her breasts. He bent to kiss each nipple, tugging on them one at a time. Then he bit into the tip, hard enough to cause pain, but not too hard to draw blood.

She gasped, her head falling back, exposing the curve of her neck, a perfect path for Jackson to follow up to her lips.

He nipped and tongued his way across the frantically beating pulse at the base of her throat and up to her mouth where he bit into her full, tender lips, tugging gently. She tasted of mint toothpaste and sex. Jackson's cock swelled tighter, anxious to plunge into her moist depths.

"Eh-hmm." Luke cleared his throat, his hand on his engorged dick.

"I'm getting there," Jackson growled. "I'm calling the shots, remember?"

Mark edged in. "You got that right. Move over Luke. I can take a little direction better than you can."

Kiki smiled at Jackson. "What would you like me to do first? Or should I say who?"

"I'm going to fuck you," he said, his voice hoarse, caught up in the raw sensuality of what was about to take place. "And while I fuck your cunt, my brother Luke will fuck you in the ass." He waited to see if she'd shy away from his demand, praying she wouldn't. If she said crackerjack, he'd back off immediately.

Her eyes widened and her tongue swept across her lips, her gaze darting from Jackson to Luke and back. "Is it possible?"

"I've never done it, but we're about to find out." He pointed to the floor. "Lie down."

Luke hesitated, scratching his head. "I don't know about this. I mean, I like my brother, but isn't that putting us a little too close? I'm not into guys and definitely not into my brother."

"But you're into me, aren't you?" Kiki lay on her side on the floor, a smile curling her lips. She nodded toward Jackson. "Luke, if you don't, I won't. Jackson is the master." She patted her bottom. "Or is it that you're afraid of a little anal sex?"

Luke shook his head, a grin stretching across his face. "Hell no." He jerked his jeans down his legs, kicking them to the side, then dropped to the floor behind Kiki and pulled her bottom toward his hard dick.

"Not yet." Jackson sucked in a deep breath. He'd never been with a woman while with other men, least of all while his brothers watched or participated. Kiki, or Audrey—whoever the hell she pretended to be—was his first shared woman. "I'm going in first.

He shed his shirt slowly, familiar with disrobing in front of his brothers, but not in front of a woman *and* his brothers. They'd skinny-dipped a number of times in the creek, so seeing each other naked wasn't new. Naked and aroused, now that was a different story. He toed off his boots, stripped his jeans and kicked them to the side. His shoulders straightened, his cock jutting forward, hard, thick and ready for Kiki. As the master, he made the next move.

He dropped to his knees in front of Kiki, his cock dangling over her face. "Touch me."

She reached out and caressed his cock. "Like this?"

"Faster."

Her hand circled him, her grip strong but soothing as she fucked him with her hand.

Jackson's groin tightened, the warmth and friction driving him deeper into this fantasy. "Enough." He grabbed her wrist, bringing her movements to a halt.

"You didn't like it?" She pouted. "Was I bad?"

"No, you were good. But I want to be inside your cunt." He lay down on his back. "Mount me."

She glanced from Mark to Luke, then slowly rose to her knees.

"You're not moving fast enough. I said mount me." He slapped her ass.

Kiki squealed and flung her knee over Jackson, the color in her cheeks high, her lips parted.

"Hey, not so rough." Mark stepped forward, fists clenched.

"No, really, it's okay. I like it…that way." She poised above Jackson's cock. "Protection?"

Luke grabbed for his jeans and dug out two condoms, handing one to Kiki and tearing one open for himself. "I was the good Boy Scout. Always prepared." He rolled the rubber down over his engorged dick.

Kiki held the package and hesitated, as if tempting Jackson's ire.

"What are you waiting for? I said mount me." Jackson pinched her tits. "Obey or suffer the consequences."

She held the foil package in her fingers, a wicked smile playing at the corner of her mouth. "And what would the consequences be?"

He slapped her ass again.

AUDREY SUCKED IN A BREATH, the sting of his hand making her hot all over, her nipples still tender from his pinch. Her pussy creamed in anticipation of being fucked by both men at the same time. She tore the package with her teeth, jerked the condom free and rolled it smoothly down his cock. Then she settled her pussy over him, his cock nudging at her entrance.

Jackson grabbed her hips and slammed her down on him, stabbing into her in one forceful thrust.

She screamed, the sound coming out before she could stop it.

Immediately Jackson lifted her up. "Are you okay?"

"Yes...yes." She tried to push herself back down on him, but he held fast. "That felt so good. Please, I want more."

"You don't want me to stop?"

"Please, *don't* stop. Fuck me." She tried to pull his hands away from her hips, but he wouldn't allow it.

"We fuck when I say we fuck, not a moment sooner." He leaned up and bit into her nipple, hard enough to elicit a twinge of pain.

Jackson wasn't Randy, Audrey had to remind herself. Had this been Randy, he wouldn't have stopped at her scream. He'd have fucked her until she bled, no matter how much she pleaded with him to stop. And Randy wouldn't be sharing her with another man, much less two.

Audrey's chest swelled with something she hadn't felt in a long time. Something she was more afraid of than pain. She refused to put a name to it, for fear the magic of this evening would be lost if she did.

"Please make love to me," she whispered.

The hard lines of Jackson's face softened, and he eased himself into her. "You know I am the master."

"Yes. You are the master." She stared down at him. "Because I let you."

He nodded acquiescence, his jaw firming. "My brother Mark is waiting patiently for some attention."

"Hey, what about me?" Luke lay on his side on the floor, propped up on his elbow. "I thought I was going in for anal sex."

"I have been remiss." Jackson shook his head. "Spank me, Kiki." He rolled to the side, presenting his butt.

Audrey blinked. "Me?"

Jackson stared hard at her over his shoulder. "Your name is Kiki, isn't it?"

She gulped and nodded slowly, the lie lodging in her throat. This was new to her. Randy had always been the Dom. She'd never been on the distributing end of the punishment. She'd always been on the receiving end. She swallowed hard and slapped Jackson's ass, the sound much louder than the sting on her hand.

A thrill shivered through her, and her pussy creamed around Jackson's cock.

"Not hard enough, woman." Jackson rolled to his back and, reaching around her, smacked her bottom, the pain so sharp it nearly brought tears to her eyes. "Do it like that." Again, he presented his ass.

Audrey's breasts tingled, her body lighting up with delicious sensations, all running rampant and spiraling down to her core. Her breathing grew ragged and she tried to shimmy down over Jackson's cock to relieve some of the sexual achiness.

"No," he said. "I didn't give you permission to fuck me. Spank me right."

A surge of impatience raged through her and she smacked Jackson's naked butt so hard her hand tingled. A small red handprint barely showed against his dark Native American skin.

"Yeah, baby! She got it right that time." Mark rubbed his hands together, a grin spilling across his face. "I've always wanted Jackson to be on the receiving end of the punishment."

"No kidding," Luke agreed.

Jackson shook his head. "I'm the master."

"Uh, right." Mark wiped the smile off, but couldn't erase the twinkle from his eyes.

"Now, give my brother Mark a blow job, while I eat you." He lifted her off his cock and positioned her pussy over his face.

"Yes, sir." Audrey reached out eagerly for Mark's member, guiding him into her mouth.

As her lips closed around Mark's shaft, Jackson's tongue thrust into her pussy.

Audrey gasped around the thick cock, her body lighting up.

Jackson swirled his tongue around her already-wet entrance and traced a line up to her clit, flicking it until she squirmed.

She sank lower, wanting more. At the same time Mark pushed deeper, his penis bumping against the back of her throat. He gently laced his fingers into her hair, moving her head back and forth to the rhythm of his thrusts.

Jackson's mouth left her clit and Audrey nearly cried out, so close to the edge of orgasm she could practically taste it.

"Luke, I can't reach Kiki's breasts, they seem to need attention." Jackson's words blew warm air across Audrey's cunt.

"Yes, Master," Luke said with laughter in his voice. He straddled Jackson, positioning himself behind her, and dropped to his knees. His cock pressed into her buttocks and his hands came up around her, cupping her breasts.

Audrey almost passed out from the barrage of sensations. Her breath caught in her throat each time one of the men touched her in a different way. The more Mark tugged on her hair, the more the pins holding the wig tugged at her scalp, adding pain to the other delectable sensations. When she thought she couldn't stand it any longer, she cried out.

"Do not come," Jackson commanded, removing his tongue from her clit. "You do not have my permission to come. Not until I tell you."

Mark pulled his cock free, coming into his hand.

"I can't help it," she whimpered. "I have to."

He cupped her pussy, applying pressure. "Wait."

Luke stood and moved aside.

Jackson slid her down his body, positioning her pussy over his cock. "We aren't finished yet." He slammed into her, driving deep and sure into her wet channel. He eased her torso down over him, thrusting into her again and again. He stopped suddenly and held her hips still. "Luke?"

"Yes, sir? Is it my turn?"

"Now." Jackson parted his thighs.

Luke slid between them on his knees and leaned over Audrey's back. "Just say the word and I'll stop."

"Please, please, just do it." She gasped, her body shaking with the intensity of her passion.

Luke's cock pressed against one of her butt cheeks while he wet his fingers with her juices. He swirled the creamy liquid around her asshole and thrust a finger into the rigid circle.

"Whew, tight," she whispered.

"Is it too much?" Jackson asked, his voice low, insistent.

"No." She sucked in a breath and relaxed her muscles, the thickness of Jackson's cock inside her making her more confident. "Please, more."

Luke removed the finger, swirled more juices around her anus and thrust in two fingers, then three.

Each time, Audrey gasped, the pain easing to a delightful ache. "Please, fuck me, please," she cried, ready for more and unwilling to wait.

Jackson's gaze shifted from her face to the man behind her. He nodded. "Gently."

Luke nudged his cock against her anus and slid in.

"Oh, dear God." Audrey thought she would come apart, the cock in her ass so tight, pressing against the dick in her pussy. "No one move."

She lay still for a moment, absorbing the pain, letting her body adjust, her channels stretching to accommodate the ample girth of two very well-hung men. As the pain abated, she nodded. "Okay, I'm okay."

Jackson slid slowly out, then back in. He waited while Luke did the same. They settled into an alternating rhythm.

Audrey lay there, unable to move for the amount of fucking and loving every minute of it. So much so that she didn't want to come, didn't want the men to come. She wanted them to continue on until she died of ecstasy.

Luke's hands on her sides tightened, his fingers digging into her skin. He pushed deeper, holding steady, his body tensing against her bottom. "Geez!" His cock pulsed inside her ass.

Her body throbbed in unison.

When Luke's grip loosened, he slid out and moved away. "Wow. That's all I can say." He shook his head, his eyes wide. "Wow."

With only Jackson buried inside her now, some of the tension left Audrey.

"Are you ready to come?"

"No." She pressed her lips to his.

"Do you want me to get you there?"

"Yes, Master. Please." She bit into his lip and tugged on it.

His arm slipped around her, and he flipped her onto her back without losing the connection. "Mark, get the ropes I keep by the back door. Oh, and the riding crop."

"Ropes? Riding crop?" Her body quickened, her breathing short and shallow. Just when she thought she had Jackson figured out, he surprised her. But ropes meant he'd have complete control. A knot of fear clenched in her gut even as a ripple of excitement fanned out across her body.

CHAPTER EIGHT

*J*ackson had never been into this Dom-sub stuff. He didn't know if he was doing it right. Hell, he could barely spell BDSM, but if that was what turned Audrey on, he was willing to try anything.

He had to admit, having his brothers participate had been a complete turn-on. Not that he was into his brothers, but watching Audrey with them and them with her—he got hard just thinking about it.

Audrey was different from any other woman Jackson had ever dated. In her work environment, she was tough as nails and didn't take shit from anyone. A huge contrast from her sex life. She wanted to be dominated, yet she wanted an out. Multiple partners made her even hotter.

The man's man inside Jackson had balked at first to sharing any woman with any other man. He wanted a woman to love him and only him. But this woman was special. She had needs and desires so intense he wondered if one man would ever be enough for her.

Was he willing to play second fiddle for long? Was there a chance at a long-term relationship with this woman? He didn't know where this would lead, but he did know he was about to throw bondage into the bag of tricks and see how she reacted.

Mark scrambled out of the room to fetch the riding crop and ropes.

Jackson leaned over Audrey and kissed her, all of his hopes and desires taking the kiss past a pleasant pressure to a joining of the hearts. He thrust past her teeth, his tongue circling hers, stroking, tasting.

When Mark returned carrying a wad of ropes and a thin black riding crop, Jackson broke the kiss and pulled his cock free of her channel. The night air cooled the heat of her moisture clinging to his skin, but not for long. He had plans to be back inside her, very soon.

She pouted up at him. "Are we done?"

"Hardly." He bent and scooped her into his arms, lifting her high.

Her arms draped around his neck, the chaps flapping against his belly, her breasts within reach of his mouth.

Jackson couldn't resist. He kissed one, then took it between his teeth and nipped.

"Ouch!" Audrey batted at his chest. "That wasn't very nice."

"I thought it was." He smiled and carried her down the hall toward the master suite. "Mark, Luke, follow."

Obediently, his brothers trailed him into the bedroom.

Once inside, Jackson stood Audrey on her feet, his hands going to the strap holding the chaps snug against her hips. "It's time to lose these." He flicked the strap and the chaps fell to the floor. "Get on the bed."

Audrey backed up, her gaze never leaving Jackson's. When the backs of her thighs touched the mattress, she sat.

"Tie her to the posts." Jackson pressed her back against the mattress, positioning her in the center of the bed. He held her wrists while Luke tied her to the posts on the headboard. Then he held her thighs while Mark tied her ankles to the footboard posts. As he waited for Mark to finish, Jackson's fingers traced the inside length of her legs to where her pussy glistened, his groin tightening the closer he glided to the center.

Once her arms and legs were tied, Audrey lay spread-eagle on the mattress, wearing only the mask, nothing else. Every glorious inch of her was exposed for the men to see.

Audrey's eyes widened. "You aren't going to leave me here, are you?"

"Couldn't even conceive of leaving you." Jackson

crawled up onto the end of the bed, slipping between her thighs. "I haven't had my fill."

"And if I have?" she challenged.

"All you have to do is say the word," Jackson shot back at her. With his breath lodged in his chest, he hoped beyond hope she didn't call it quits now. He'd held back, refusing to come until he had her exactly where he wanted her.

"I guess I could stay a little longer." She tugged against the ropes around her wrists. "But this isn't fair. What if I want to touch?"

"Who's the master?"

Her pout deepened. "You are, damn it."

"That wasn't very nicely said." Jackson extended his hand. "Mark, the whip."

Mark handed him the whip. "Don't hurt her." He glared at his brother, his lips pressing into a stern line. "This could get out of hand really fast."

"I know what I'm doing. Either shut up or leave."

Mark's mouth tightened, but he stayed, crossing his arms over his chest, taking up a position on one side of the bed.

Luke stood on the other side, his arms also crossed, both men looking like bouncers at the Ugly Stick Saloon.

Jackson fought to keep from laughing out loud, forcing his brows together for a stern look. "The lady needs punishing."

"I do?"

"Yes." He slapped the riding crop into his open

palm, testing the impact. He had no intention of hurting her, but he knew she liked a little pain with her sex. With the crop balanced in his fingers, he ran it along the smooth skin of her calf and up the length of her outer thigh. "Who is the master?"

"You are, damn it," she said in flagrant defiance of his earlier chastisement. Her tongue swept across her lower lip, her gaze fixed on the whip in his hand, her expression hungry, not scared.

Mark laughed. "She wants him to use the whip."

Jackson popped her thigh with the tip of the crop. He trailed the end of the whip up over her flat belly to the swell of her breasts, circling each of her nipples one at a time. "Who is the master?"

"You are, damn it," she said, her voice more breathy, labored.

He tapped the crop sharply across her right nipple.

Audrey's eyes squeezed shut, her nipples beading into tight little buttons.

Mark and Luke both stepped forward, fists clenched.

Jackson held up a hand to stop them.

"Please," Audrey said. "Do it again." She opened eyes clouded with lust. "I've been so very bad."

Jackson heaved a sigh at the same time as his brothers. Everything with Audrey was a new experience, a path uncharted. He dragged the whip across her breasts, nipple to nipple, and down to her bellybutton.

Her head lifted, her gaze following the crop. "Please, Master. Please."

"Please what?" Jackson asked, the crop circling her bellybutton.

"Lower. Oh God, lower."

"Oh, for Pete's sake." Mark leaped forward and grabbed for the whip. "Let me."

Jackson held tight and growled, "Back off."

For a moment the two glared at each other, then Mark stepped back, letting go of the riding crop.

Jackson looked up at Audrey. "Who do you want to guide the whip?"

She stared straight into his eyes. "You, Master."

With a nod, he lightly breezed over her skin to the curly thatch of strawberry-blonde hair at the juncture of her thighs. He flicked the hairs, parting them, pushing deeper to the folds beneath. Once he had the rod of the crop against her clitoris, he sawed it gently back and forth.

Audrey's back arched off the bed, her knees pulling in, her ankles halting her progress. "Please, oh, please."

"How does that make you feel?"

"Like I'm on fire. Please let me touch you. If not, let me touch my breasts," she begged, looking up hopefully.

"You want to be touched?" Jackson nodded to Luke and Mark. "You heard the lady, touch her breasts."

Luke and Mark sprang forward. Luke rolled

Audrey's nipple between his thumb and forefinger. Mark bent and licked the areola, drawing a circle with his tongue before he sucked the whole thing into his mouth, pulling so hard his cheeks sank in.

Audrey pressed into him.

Not to be outdone, Luke bent over her and took her other nipple between his teeth and nibbled, then sucked.

Confident she was being taken care of, Jackson continued his attack. "Do you like what my brothers are doing?"

"Yesss," she cried, her body undulating against the sheets.

He slapped the inside of her thigh with the riding crop.

Audrey gasped.

"Yes, what?" Jackson asked.

"Yes, Master."

He swished the tip of the crop over the red mark it had left, then dragged it up to her moist pussy, swirling the end in her juices. He laid down between her legs and buried his face in her bush, tonguing her clit while he used the tip of the riding crop to stroke her entrance. His mouth moved lower, his tongue darting into her channel, lapping at her creamy center. From her pussy to her clit, he alternated, until her cries became louder, her body bucking from all of the attention.

When she suddenly stiffened, he knew he had her where he wanted her.

His cock couldn't get any harder and he could wait no longer.

"Get back," he ordered his brothers.

Mark and Luke jumped back as Jackson climbed between Audrey's legs, lifted her hips and plunged into her.

"Faster," she screamed.

Jackson popped her leg with the crop. "Faster what?"

"Faster, Master!" she shouted.

He rode her faster.

"Harder."

He tapped her nipple.

"Harder, Master. Pleeease!"

The bedframe groaned and creaked as Jackson thrust into Audrey, again and again, his balls hitting her skin making a clapping sound between the grunts and heavy breathing.

Audrey grasped the ropes binding her wrists, pulling hard to leverage her hips upward to meet him thrust for thrust.

Every muscle in Jackson's body tensed, every nerve exploding in a firestorm of orgasm, shooting him over the precipice into an abyss so wonderful, he never wanted to return. He rammed in and out, his cock hot with friction.

At the crest of his climax, he called out, "Audrey!" his eyes squeezing shut with the power of his release.

It took several minutes for his mind to reengage,

and when it did, an eerie silence had settled over the room.

Mark and Luke stood back, their eyes wide.

Jackson's gaze shot to Audrey, and it finally struck him what he'd done.

Tears rolled from the corners of her eyes, dampening the fabric of the black mask. Her voice no more than a whisper, Audrey said, "Crackerjack."

Mark and Luke moved forward, working to loosen the ropes at her wrists.

Jackson slid out of her and off the end of the bed, his fingers fumbling with the bindings at her ankles.

He didn't look up until she was completely free. Red marks on her wrists and ankles served as a reminder of their journey.

Audrey rolled to the side, dragging the sheet with her.

"Audrey." Jackson reached to pull her into his arms.

She sidestepped him and ran from the bedroom.

Luke shook his head. "I had no idea."

Jackson went after her.

Mark slammed an arm across his chest before he could leave the bedroom. "Let her go."

Jackson shoved at Mark. "I can't."

"She said the word. You have to."

Jackson's footsteps faltered. He'd promised he would stop everything if she said her safe word. He balanced back and forth on the balls of his bare feet and then shot forward. He couldn't let her go like this.

Before he could catch up with her, she'd left, the blonde wig and the black mask lying in the dirt.

An engine roared behind the house and her bright red pickup barreled around the corner, kicking up gravel.

"Audrey!" Jackson ran toward the truck.

She swerved around him and gunned the accelerator, rocketing down the driveway, away from the Gray Wolf Ranch and out of Jackson's life.

AUDREY SWIPED at the tears flowing down her face. She couldn't seem to make them stop. They came in waves, gushing out with her sobs, blinding her to the road ahead. She couldn't slow the vehicle. Not until she got far enough away Jackson couldn't find her.

Assuming he would even come after her.

What an idiot she'd been to think she could fool Jackson. How long had he known? Why hadn't he called her bluff before they'd gone so far? Had he been using her? Just like Randy had used her?

Deep down, she knew Jackson's treatment of her hadn't been anything like Randy's, but still. He'd known who she was, known she was hiding. Why hadn't he told her? Why?

Audrey turned onto a deserted road and pulled behind a broad oak tree, hoping any passerby on the main highway would miss her and keep going. Even before she shifted into park, the sobs rose in earnest, the tears flowing like rivers.

She should never have taken the job to dance for the Gray Wolf brothers. Hell, she should never have fucked Jackson in the storeroom. If she'd remained committed to her battery-powered toys, she wouldn't be faced with this mess, this drama. Now what should she do?

When the storm abated, Audrey scrubbed her face with the napkins she kept in her console. Any makeup she'd applied prior to performing for the brothers was long gone, leaving only red-rimmed, bloodshot eyes staring back at her in the visor mirror.

Hell, it couldn't be helped. Who cared anyway?

She pulled back out on the road and headed for Temptation. She could lock herself in her house and refuse to come out for days. As she blew past the turn-off to the Ugly Stick, she shook her head.

No. She had a business to run. So, she'd taken a step on the wild side, exploring her sexual fantasies of multiple partners. She'd broken the promise she'd made to herself when she'd left Randy to never let a man dominate her again. Although, Jackson's domination hadn't been anything like what Randy had inflicted on her. Randy had been verbally, mentally and physically abusive.

Jackson had been ready to call it off. And he'd proven it when she'd cried out her safe word, backing away immediately, untying her and letting her go.

Then why was she so disappointed that he hadn't come after her?

Randy always came after her, dragging her back, sometimes by the hair, sometimes after a thorough beating that often left her with bruises and on occasion a broken rib.

No, her ex-boyfriend wasn't made of the same stuff as Jackson Gray Wolf. Jackson was a man who kept his promises and didn't abuse women.

And he'd known it was her all along.

As she pulled into the driveway of her cottage on the outskirts of Temptation, she leaned her forehead on her steering wheel, too tired to move, too emotionally exhausted to care.

The cell phone she'd left in the cup holder buzzed, jerking Audrey out of her pity party.

Her heart flipped over and she grabbed for the phone. Was it Jackson? Was he calling to apologize to her? Did he want her back? Despite her vow to never talk to the man again, she glanced down at the device, hope dying as the screen lit up.

The caller ID was the Ugly Stick Saloon.

Audrey almost threw the phone out the window but thought better of it. Charli wouldn't call unless it was an emergency.

With a sigh, Audrey hit the talk button. "Yeah?"

A roaring sound blasted in Audrey's ear, then

Charli shouted, "Hate to bother you so late, but I have a minor crisis here."

"What is it?"

"I can't hear you, Audrey. If you can hear me, I need you here ASAP."

"Can't—" Before she could get Charli to answer, the woman ended the call.

"Damn!" Audrey realized for the first time that she was still naked, her skin sticking to the leather of the seat. For the hundredth time since she'd purchased the cottage, she counted her blessings for the distance between her and her nearest neighbor. If she was careful, she'd get inside before they saw her naked white body streaking by. She thanked her lucky stars the cops hadn't seen her and pulled her over. Indecent exposure charges would hit the sheriff's blotter the next day and her antics would spread like wildfire.

Other than getting the front door key stuck in the lock, she made it inside, none the worse for the exposure.

Throwing on her clothes and a pair of tennis shoes, she raced back outside, jumped into her truck and hit the road toward the county line where the Ugly Stick Saloon stood. Her hands shook and she would burst into tears if anyone even looked at her cross-eyed. She was in no shape to deal with anything else tonight.

"Charli," she muttered. "This better be good."

CHAPTER NINE

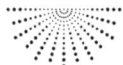

*A*udrey had a good lead on Jackson by the time he dressed and climbed into his pickup truck. Mark and Luke jumped in as he pulled out of the yard.

"You're not going without us." Luke slid into the middle seat.

Jackson's hands clenched. "I can handle this on my own."

"We got you into this," Mark said. "We can damn sure help you out."

Jackson ran his hand through his hair and stared at the road ahead. "I don't know how."

Mark chuckled. "Who'dve thunk. Our little dancer Kiki was none other than Audrey." He slapped his knee and laughed.

"It's not funny." Jackson glared at Mark. "At least not to her."

Luke grinned. "She put on a damned good show. I'd buy tickets to that any day."

Jackson groaned. "This is all my fault."

Mark and Luke stared across at him.

"How?" Luke asked. "*We* hired her."

"*I* took advantage of her, knowing Kiki was Audrey."

"How long have you known it was her?"

"I think I knew from the beginning that she was familiar, but it wasn't until I found her red boot under my bed the morning after my birthday party."

"Well, damn." Mark smacked his palm to his forehead. "I never put the red boots and Audrey together. But you're right. Audrey always wore those go-to-hell red boots. I should have seen it."

"Well, I did and I went after her knowing it was her." A knot of lead settled in the pit of Jackson's stomach.

"Nice of you to clue us in, brother." Luke crossed his arms over his chest, giving Jackson a disapproving frown.

Mark leaned forward. "Why didn't you say anything tonight?"

"I figured there was a reason she wanted to pretend to be someone else. Maybe some jerk ex-boyfriend took advantage of her...sexual appetites. Maybe this was her weird way of being in control when she let a man be in control."

Luke snorted. "Female thinkin'. I'll never understand it."

"I think our brother missed his calling." Mark nudged Luke in the chest. "Instead of wrangling cattle, he shoulda been a shrink."

"Or a sex doctor." Luke ran a hand through his hair. "Gotta say, I didn't know you had all that whips and ropes stuff in you. I always thought you were on the straight and narrow."

Jackson frowned. "What happens on the ranch—"

"We know," Luke said. "What happens on the ranch…"

"Stays on the ranch," Luke and Mark said in unison.

"But wow, what a woman." Luke smiled. "I've never met one who wanted to be shared."

Jackson's lips twisted into a wry grin. "You'd be surprised by some women's fantasies."

"And you would know about women's fantasies…*how*?" Mark laughed. "You barely date."

Jackson frowned. "I read the articles in magazines."

"Is that what you do when you hog the bathroom for hours on end?" Luke chuckled.

"Are you looking for her truck?" Jackson demanded.

"Lookin'." Luke craned his neck. "I think she got away."

As he neared the county line, Jackson had to agree with Luke. He hadn't seen her truck and probably wouldn't.

Mark tapped his knuckles on the window beside him. "Head for the Ugly Stick. She might be there."

Jackson cut to the right, the back end of the truck sliding sideways as he took the turn toward the saloon faster than he should have. Tucked back in a copse of trees, the security lights in the parking lot of the Ugly Stick Saloon were the only illumination in the darkness of the Texas night.

Clouds must have rolled in, blocking out the stars and the moonlight, making the Ugly Stick a little pocket of light.

Women exited the saloon, some staggering, most still whooping it up from the strip show the Ugly Stick provided to the ladies one night a month.

Jackson grabbed the red boot from behind his seat and pushed past the crowd lingering in the parking lot saying their goodbyes or arguing over who would drive. As he muscled his way up to the door, women paused as if sniffing the air, their eyes widening when they spotted the three men.

One reached out and touched him, running her hands across his chest. "Oh, baby, I missed this one. Which costume did you wear?" She leaned into him, her breath reeking of alcohol.

"I don't know what you're talking about, lady. Excuse me." He gently removed her hand from his chest and ducked around her.

Another woman blocked his path, dangling a dollar bill in her fingers. "Yeah, baby, let me." She shoved the bill down the front of his jeans, fondling his package before Jackson could jerk her hand free.

Mark and Luke caught up with him, grins splitting their faces in two.

Mark staggered backward when a woman flung her arms around his neck and planted a big, sloppy kiss on his face, missing his lips and sliding down his chin. He chuckled and steadied her on her feet, sending her after her designated driver. "Damn. I've never seen so many horny women."

"Did you see that?" Luke was staring after a woman. "She pinched my ass."

"You're lucky that's all she pinched." Jackson tightened his belt and pushed through the entryway.

The women inside were no easier on them. As soon as Jackson cleared the doorway, a woman grabbed his T-shirt, stretching it so far he had to duck out of it to get away from her. When she jerked off his shirt, the boot flew across the room. Jackson dove for it.

He might as well have started a riot. Once the other women saw his naked chest, every female in the establishment screamed and crowded in on the three men, ripping shirts, grabbing for pant legs and belt buckles.

Trapped on his knees in the melee, Jackson could do nothing. He couldn't hit them—they were women. One woman reached around him and unbuckled his belt, another unzipped his jeans and several had a hold of his boots, tugging them off with surprising strength. Jackson held tightly to his jeans with one hand and to the red boot with the other. But he wasn't strong enough to ward off a dozen women pulling at his jeans like a tug-of-war rope.

Off they came, half a dozen women falling over like dominoes.

Jackson leaped to his socked feet and tried to make a dash for the bar.

"Oh lucky day! He's not even wearing a G-string!"

Women screamed and charged after him, hands groping, spinning him around so that they too could see his goddamn dick. He tried to be nice, tried not to hurt anyone, but he was getting fuckin' tired of being treated like a prize bull at a cattle auction—poked and prodded like fresh meat.

He caught a glimpse of Mark and Luke. Damned if his brothers weren't enjoying all the attention.

Mark spun his T-shirt over his head and let it fly.

Luke stood flexing his muscles for a crowd of women of all ages, each vying for a chance to get close enough to run their hands across his dark skin.

Jackson just wanted to get to Audrey. He spotted Charli in the distance climbing onto the bar.

"Hey, ladies, calm down." She put her fingers to her lips and whistled, loud enough to pierce Jackson's eardrums. "These men aren't part of the show."

The crowd quieted for a moment until one woman shouted, "They are now. Finders keepers!"

The frenzy recommenced. No amount of ear-splitting whistles would stop the rabid, horny women from clawing, kissing, pinching and grabbing the men.

Jackson's heart hammered as he struggled one agonizing step at a time, inching his way through the throng toward the bar. His ass hurt from all the pinching, and some women even pinched his dick.

Animals!

Once he reached the relative safety of the bar, he hauled himself up on the wooden platform, dragging in deep gulps of air.

As soon as he straightened, the noise level skyrocketed.

"Oh, baby, he's gonna dance!"

"Crank up the music."

"Dang, he's hung like a horse!"

"I want me some of that."

Mark reached the bar about the time the music started, Luke seconds after.

They too had been stripped of boots, hats, shirts and belts. Unlike their big brother, they still wore their jeans.

Mark laughed up at Jackson. "You got balls, bro."

"Shut the fuck up." Jackson scanned the crowd. "Do you see my jeans anywhere?"

"No." Mark hauled himself up on the bar, but hands grabbed his legs and he was forced to sit instead of stand. More hands grasped his jeans and pulled. He held on to the edge of the bar to keep from falling off. He fought valiantly, but his jeans lost the war and were flung high above the crowd.

Luke shook his head, backing against the bar. "No way." He waved his hands in front of the ladies. "I'm keeping my jeans." With his thumbs hooked through his belt loops, he fought to maintain his hold. Then his legs were ripped out from under him. Luke made a grab for the bar, barely catching the edge before his legs were dragged out behind him, forcing him to levitate above the concrete floor. The jeans slipped off, and he too scrambled to stand out of reach of pinching fingers groping his privates.

Jackson would have laughed out loud, but he was too busy holding off the hordes, bracing the red boot in front of him over his shriveling cock.

The music came on, the sound rising enough to be heard over the screams. Women stopped grabbing and started clapping in time, and soon a chant raised the roof. "Dance! Dance! Dance!"

Charli had disappeared into the back room, reemerging as the chanting began.

"Did you call the sheriff?" Jackson shouted over the noise.

Charli grinned and pointed to her ears, mouthing the words, *Can't hear you.* Before Jackson could ask again, even Charli was clapping her hands and chanting, her gaze raking over Jackson's, Mark's and Luke's bodies, pausing at the most vulnerable spots.

Jackson groaned. He couldn't get off the bar or his privates would be so violated he might never sire children. All he could do was wait out the storm and hope the women got bored and left soon.

Mark and Luke swayed to the music, flexing their muscles and grinding their hips.

Cries rose from the ladies, and they shouted, "More!"

At the back of the crowd a glimpse of strawberry-blonde hair caught Jackson's eye like a ray of hope in a stormy sky. Was it...?

A woman made a grab for the red boot he held in front of his dick and jerked it out of his hand. "We want to see."

Jackson lunged for the boot, falling into the crowd. Like a rock star at a concert, they moved him above their heads, touching, feeling and fondling all the way.

He spotted the red boot on the floor near some-one's feet, and he rolled to the side, disrupting the chain of hands. He dropped to the floor, lunged for the boot, and it was whisked out of sight before he could get his hands on it. He straightened, his gaze climbing the denim-clad legs to face off with Greta Sue, the female bouncer. In her hand, she held the boot. "Looking for this?"

Jackson smiled and winced as the woman behind him reached between his legs and squeezed his scrotum.

Greta Sue glared at the woman. "Back off, bitch."

The woman let go of Jackson's balls and stepped back.

Straightening to his full height, Jackson squared off with Greta Sue. "Yes. I was looking for that."

She inspected the boot. "Not your size."

A hand snaked out from behind Greta Sue and plucked the boot from her fingers. "No, but it's mine." Audrey's voice carried over the roar of the crowd.

Jackson's heart thundered against his ribs. This was not the way he envisioned this meeting would go. He fought the urge to fig-leaf his hand over his penis. She'd seen it all, touched it and fucked it. That last thought put life into his limp dick. Ah, hell, the more he tried not to think about all they'd done, the more he did and the bigger his cock swelled.

Several women standing nearby gasped.

One touched her throat and cried, "Oh, my." Fingers stretched out to touch his member.

Greta Sue blocked her hand. "Don't touch the merchandise."

Jackson grinned at her. "Thanks."

"Thanks, nothing. I want a clear view, not some skanky female's hands all over, blocking that masterpiece."

"Greta Sue," Audrey said in a quiet, authoritative voice. "I'll take it from here."

Greta Sue grunted. "I just bet you will." The big woman moved to the side, clearing the path between Audrey and Jackson.

Audrey's brows rose, her gaze skimming him from head to foot. "Lose something?"

He shrugged, forcing a nonchalance he didn't feel standing naked in front of a hundred drooling women. "More like I found something."

She glanced at her boot. "Wondered where it had gotten to. Thanks for returning it." Audrey nodded toward the bouncer. "Greta Sue will escort you and your brothers out, when you're quite through entertaining the ladies." She spun and strode for the door behind the bar.

"Audrey!" he yelled.

Audrey didn't appear to notice, didn't turn and acknowledge him or anything. Well, hell!

Jackson tried to follow her, but the crowd closed in on him again, blocking his path. He glanced at Greta Sue. "Help me."

Greta grinned. "Whatcha gonna give me?"

He stared around the room. What could he give this woman? Everything he'd worn into the room had been stripped from his body. All he had was himself. With a grin, he waved at his cock and shrugged. "A good grope?"

"Deal." She strong-armed her way through the grasping, pinching women, clearing a path for him to reach the bar. Then she gave him a boost up to join his brothers.

With a deep breath, he turned to face Greta Sue. "Go ahead."

Greta Sue reached out a meaty hand and ran her fingers gently along his cock from the tip to the base, then fondled his balls, threading her fingers through the dark hairs.

It could have been worse. Those hands could have

crushed juice from an avocado seed. Jackson counted himself lucky that he'd gotten off so easy.

Greta Sue sighed. "Thanks, hun." Then she disappeared into the crowd.

Jackson turned toward the door leading into the back-office area and storeroom. Audrey stood there, a sad smile curling her lips.

"Audrey." Jackson held out a hand to her.

She shook her head, her eyes shining suspiciously. When she spun away, Jackson knew he had to do something radical to get her attention.

He shouted above the ladies' screams. "Wanna see me dance?"

Every woman in the building gave a resounding, "*Hell, yeah!*"

He crossed his arms over his chest and jerked his head toward Audrey's retreating figure. "I will, only if Audrey Anderson stays to watch."

A surge of women shoved through the door where Audrey had disappeared, emerging seconds later with the struggling bar owner.

"What are you doing?" she cried.

"He's gonna dance, but you have to watch too." Greta Sue hooked Audrey's arm and marched her forward.

"I'm dedicating this dance to a fun-loving, sexy woman I'd love to get to know so much better." Jackson nodded to the woman at the jukebox. "Play something hot and sexy."

Music filled the air and shouts rose to the ceiling,

fading away so that they could hear the music as Jackson swayed and ground his hips, dancing across the bar toward Audrey.

As he neared her, she backed away.

Mark and Luke leaped off the bar and blocked her escape, their bodies pressing into hers, their cocks fully engorged.

"I think I'm in love," a woman wailed.

"With which one?" the woman next to her asked.

"All of them. Look at the size of those cocks." She fanned herself.

Jackson ignored the comments, his gaze and attention solely focused on one woman. He'd never been much for dancing, and was probably doing it wrong, but he wanted to give back some of what she'd given him. He danced for Audrey.

Halfway through the song, Jackson slipped off the bar and landed in front of Audrey. "Don't run away from me, beautiful lady. Please. I'm baring my soul to you in this dance."

Luke snorted. "That's not the only thing he's baring."

"Yeah," Mark added. "We came to find you."

Tears welled in Audrey's eyes, and she raised her hand to wipe them away. "I'm not that other person."

Jackson grabbed her wrist, bringing her hand to his lips. "Yes, you are."

"No." She looked up, her blue eyes awash with moisture. "I can't be that person ever again."

"Maybe not, but you can be yourself." Jackson laid

her hand on his chest. "Feel how hard you make my heart beat?"

She nodded, tears slipping down her cheeks now. "But—"

He pressed a finger to her lips and replaced it with his mouth. "We love you just the way you are, in boots and chaps or nothing at all. *I* love you just the way you are."

Audrey glanced away from Jackson, unable to look into his eyes. Unable to believe the tenderness she saw there. Randy had made her feel that her desires were wrong, wicked and dirty.

Weren't they?

The shouting had stopped, the entire room growing silent, every ear turned toward Jackson, Audrey and the twins.

"Who could love someone like that?" she whispered.

Jackson lifted her chin and stared down into her eyes. "I could, if you'd let me."

"And me," Luke chimed in.

Mark tucked a strand of her strawberry-blonde hair behind her ear. "Me too."

Audrey laughed, the sound catching on a sob. "Really?"

Jackson pulled her into his arms, his warmth wiping away the coldness of her past, the worry that she was unworthy to be loved by a man, much less three.

A collective sigh rose from the crowd and a soft chanting rose to fill the silence. *"Kiss her."*

Jackson tipped Audrey's chin, and when his lips pressed against hers, his cock nudged her belly, stirring to life the desires she'd unleashed only a short time ago. Her hands rounded his waist and dropped to his buttocks, pulling him closer.

"So unfair," she whispered against his lips.

"What's unfair?" He brushed his mouth across her nose, her eyes, her cheekbone.

Audrey breathed deeply, letting go of the last of her inhibitions, the final ghosts that had haunted her for the past few years, and smiled up at Jackson. "You're naked and I'm not."

Jackson bent, scooped her into his arms and carried her through the door into the storeroom where it had all begun.

Mark and Luke whooped and followed, closing the door behind them.

When they had the room to themselves, the men gently stripped Audrey of her clothes and one by one, they touched her, letting her know they could be as gentle as they could be rough, as tender as they were kinky.

Jackson took center stage, lifting her to wrap her legs around his waist. "Your desires are my desires. If you want multiple partners, you've got it."

"What about spanking?" she asked, wiggling, trying to sheathe him with her cunt and failing miserably. He wouldn't let her lower herself over him. "Do you think a business owner should like to be spanked?"

Jackson grinned and held her above his jutting penis. "Absolutely." He smacked her ass.

Audrey squealed. "What was that for?"

With a grin, he rubbed the stinging area. "Wait until you're invited to fuck me."

Mark stood behind her, his hands cupping her breasts, pinching the nipples hard enough to make her squirm. "Do you like that?"

"Ummm, yes." She leaned back against him. "Do it again."

He did.

Luke caressed her ass, his finger finding and poking into her anus. "And this?"

Her breathing came in shallow gulps. "Yes."

Jackson lifted her higher, positioning her pussy directly over his dick.

The anticipation was killing Audrey. She wanted Jackson inside her so badly she might burst into yet another round of tears. What was wrong with her? She never cried.

"Please." She grabbed his cheeks and forced him to stare into her eyes. "Please. I can't take much more. Fuck me, Master."

"I love it when you beg." He kissed her and plunged into her, his cock spearing her, thrusting deep, hard and rough.

Just the way she liked it.

BOOTS & SEX ED

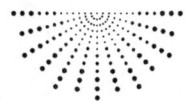

UGLY STICK SALOON BOOK #2

New York Times & USA Today
Bestselling Author
ELLE JAMES

writing as

MYLA JACKSON

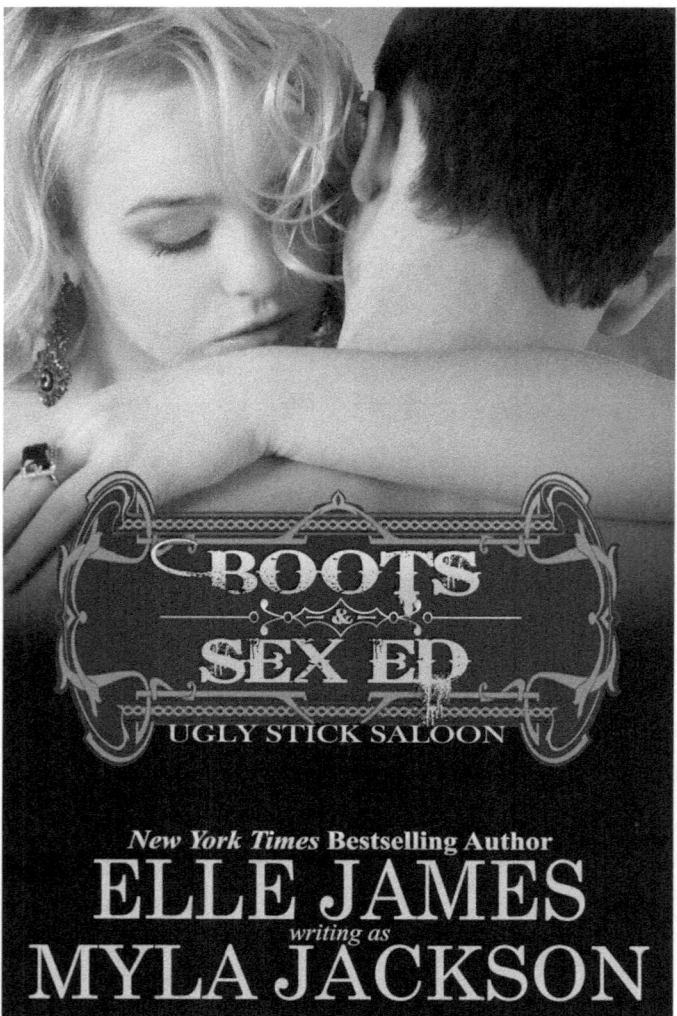

BOOTS
&
SEX ED

UGLY STICK SALOON

New York Times Bestselling Author
ELLE JAMES
writing as
MYLA JACKSON

CHAPTER ONE

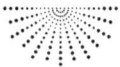

*E*dward Judson slapped his dusty cowboy hat against his leg as he led his black gelding into the barn. The sun baked the weathered boards of the exterior, while the interior remained relatively cool. It took a few moments for his eyes to adjust to the shadows. "I traded that stock yesterday, made enough to pay off my land and put a hefty chunk of cash down on a house."

"Good move." Grant Fowler slung a leg over the pinto mare and dropped to the ground.

Ed owed Grant a lot for teaching him everything he knew about trading shares on the stock market. The man owned a 5,000-acre ranch for a reason. Not because he was good at raising horses, but because he was damned good at managing money.

"You don't need my advice anymore, Ed," Grant said. "You could go into financial planning yourself with a few courses for certification."

"Not interested." Ed had just begun to understand the stock market's full potential and seeing the fruits of his trades pay off. But he didn't need a lot of money, just enough for his own purposes.

"You gonna work training horses for other people like me the rest of your life?"

"Nope." Ed grinned. "Not that I don't appreciate the work and all, but I got plans of my own."

"Whatcha gonna do with two hundred acres, Ed?"

"Get married someday, settle down, raise a family and some horses. It's what I'm good at." He shifted his boots in the loose dirt of the barn floor. "The horses part."

"You're good at day-trading, dude."

"I'll do that on the side so that I can afford my horses too."

Grant shook his head, a smile spreading across his face. "Okay, I get it. Can't say that I blame you. At least when you're trading for yourself, you don't have the responsibility of other people's money hanging over you."

"You hit the nail on the head."

"So how is babysitting Connor Mason's sister? Saw her at the Ugly Stick Saloon last night." Grant whistled. "Looks to me like you got yourself a hot little handful in that one."

Ed's muscles tightened, his pulse kicking up a notch as he stepped around the end of the stall. "What do you mean?"

Grant held up his hands. "Nothing, buddy. Not a thing. Just that she's a pretty girl."

"Yeah and every man in the building was drooling over her. I get it. Don't add to the crowd, will ya?" He should never have offered to look out for Kendall Mason. Especially now that she was over twenty-one and legal in every way. As far as Ed was concerned, her body should be considered a class-one felony.

Every time he looked at her, he wanted to commit all kinds of lewd and lascivious acts. With two hard pulls, he yanked the leather strap from the girth around the horse's belly and let it fall, swinging to the other side.

Grant leaned on his saddle, apparently in no hurry whatsoever to groom his own horse or end the current conversation. "I don't see how you do it."

"Do what?" As far as Ed was concerned, Grant talked too much. If he wasn't the boss, he'd probably tell him so. Hell, he might anyway.

"I don't know how you can keep your hands off her."

For the past six months, Ed had been fighting that very urge. "Grant, you talk too much." His hands ached to get hold of Kendall and touch her in ways that had nothing to do with brotherly love.

Grant laughed out loud, then continued to rub it in.

Much to Ed's agony.

"With that body and those boobs, the temptation would kill me."

"Resist, or I might just have to kill you. And I'd hate to lose my job because I killed the boss." Ed tossed the saddle onto a nearby saddle rack and grabbed a brush from the shelf, eager to get the task done and get home.

When Grant made no move to remove his horse's saddle, it was all Ed could do not to throw the brush at the man. With quick, calming strokes, Ed curried his gelding, refusing to respond to any other conversation from Grant.

"Okay, okay, I get the hint." Grant finally turned toward his saddle and removed the strap around the horse's belly. "I'm just saying you're a better man than I am."

Ed snorted. As he ran the brush over the horse's hindquarters, his cell phone vibrated his back pocket. He pulled it out and clicked the talk button. "Yeah."

"Ed?"

Every red blood cell leaped to attention at the sound of Kendall's voice. Then they all sped south to pool in his groin. Grant had it right. Keeping his hands off Kendall was only half his problem. Keeping his mind off her had become an impossibility.

"What do you need Kendall?"

"When are you coming home? I have a project I need your help on."

"I'm not much good with school projects. Get one of your classmates to help you out."

"I would, but I'd rather you help me on this one. It's special and you're my best choice," her breath whooshed out slowly before she continued, "the only man I trust."

Ed sucked in a deep breath, his imagination running rampant over the close quarters they'd be working in. He couldn't do it. No way. *Just tell her.* "I'll be home in fifteen minutes."

"Oh, good. I'll be waiting," she whispered into his ear, and the phone went silent.

Ed had a good start on a full-blown erection by the time he climbed into his truck and turned it toward Temptation, Texas, the little backwater town he'd been born and raised in.

The short ride home from the Rockin' G Ranch wasn't nearly long enough to cool the heat building in his loins. Tomorrow, he'd start looking for a different place to live. He'd planned on living in the apartment below Kendall's until he had his own house built, but the way things were going, the way he felt about his best friend's little sister...He couldn't last much longer without doing something stupid.

As he turned onto the street where the old Ross house stood, a convertible backed out of the driveway he shared with the other two occupants. A muscular, bare-chested young man smiled and waved as he passed by with the top down, his long, bright blond hair blowing in the breeze.

His fingers tightened on the steering wheel and a frown settled between Ed's brows. Who the hell was that leaving the house he shared with Kendall and Lacey? Better be one of Lacey's conquests. She was old enough to manage her own affairs. Kendall, on the other hand, had barely been twenty-one for a few weeks. She'd better not be messing around on Ed's watch.

As he shifted into park, he glanced up at the window to Kendall's apartment. The blinds were open and Kendall stood with her side to the window, wearing nothing but a thin, lace bra and thong panties. She turned her back to the window and unclipped the bra, letting it fall down over her arms to the floor.

She might as well be naked—the thin strap of the thong cutting a line between her butt cheeks hid nothing.

Ed moaned, his cock twitched, and blood rushed in to make it swell behind his zipper. He forced anger to follow the powerful rush of lust. Did the girl have so little sense as to leave her window wide open so that any peeping Tom could look in?

With the storm of lust and righteous anger driving him forward, Ed leaped out of the car, passed the door to his apartment on the first floor and took the steps two at a time to the upper apartment where Kendall lived. He hammered on the door until Kendall flung it open.

"Oh, Ed." She cupped her hands over her naked breasts, like that did anything to hide their beautiful, lush fullness from Ed's vision. "Where's the fire?"

Ed pushed past her and marched to the window on the other side of the apartment, yanking the string on the shade so hard, the shade popped out of its slot and clattered to the floor.

Kendall giggled behind him, her eyes going wide when Ed glared.

He gathered the shade from the floor, fit the ends into the slot and lowered it with more precision and care this time. When he was done, he faced Kendall, and breathed a sigh to find her clutching a shirt to her chest. "Don't undress in front of the window. I thought your mother taught you better than that."

"There's not anyone on this street who'd care but Old Man Frantzen." She tossed her hair. "I'm sure he's so blind he couldn't see that far anyway."

Ed jerked his thumb toward the window. "You never know what perverts are lurking out there looking for an eyeful. And honey, you were giving an eyeful and then some."

Her eyelids closed to half-mast and she sidled close. "Perverts? Hum…sounds interesting." Slim fingers climbed up his chest and the shirt she held slipped lower, letting one perky nipple peek through.

Ed reached out and lifted the shirt to cover her flesh, realizing his mistake as soon as the backs of his fingers brushed over her naked skin. Stifling a groan, he jumped back. "Just close the blinds before you strip, will ya?"

"Yes, sir!" Kendall popped a salute.

That pesky shirt slipped down again to expose the other pretty breast.

A moan escaped Ed's throat and he dove for the door.

Kendall stood at her door as Ed beat a hasty retreat down the steps to his apartment. No sooner had his door slammed than Lacey's door opened across the hall from Kendall.

"Well?" Lacey pushed Kendall into her apartment and closed the door behind her. "How'd it go?"

"I don't know." Kendall frowned. "He came in all angry and left like a cat with his tail on fire."

Lacey's face split in a grin. "Did you show him some boobs?"

Heat flooded Kendall's cheeks. She held her tank top in front of her like she had positioned it for Ed. "I did this side first." She switched to let the other side be exposed. "I did this side and when he answered the door, all I had was this." She dropped the shirt altogether and covered her breasts with her hands.

"Did he touch them?"

"Yes, and no." Kendall's chest rose and fell on a heartfelt sigh. "Only to cover them."

"Did he mention Cory leaving with his shirt off?"

"Not a word." Kendal dropped onto the sofa. "What am I doing wrong?"

Lacey laughed out loud. "Honey, you did it all right."

"Then why isn't he taking the hint?"

"Oh, he took it all right. I'll bet he's taking a really

cold shower right now. Shh. Listen." Lacey cupped her fingers around her ear, a smile curling the corners of her lips. "Yup, he's in the shower." She clapped her hands together. "Now, as soon as the water shuts off, be at his door ready to launch Plan B."

"I don't know. He didn't seem too excited by the idea of me being naked."

"Of course, he isn't excited by the idea of you getting naked with anyone else. I take it he closed the blinds based on the noise I heard a minute ago?" She stood with her arms crossed.

"Yeah, so?" Kendall shrugged. "My brother would have done the same. Face it, the man has a brother complex. He can't touch me because he thinks of me as his kid sister."

"Then your job is to show him you're neither his sister, nor a kid."

The pipes clanked in the wall beside Kendall, indicating the shower had been turned off below. Kendall dragged in a deep breath and let it slowly in an attempt to slow her pulse. It didn't work.

Lacey's mouth set in a firm line. "That's your cue." She herded Kendall to the door, grabbing the tank top from the floor. "Don't be too obvious too fast, it tends to scare men off. Remember Plan B. Make him think you're after someone else. Make him jealous enough to cross the brother line. Trust me, there will be no returning."

Lacey practically shoved her down the stairs.

Halfway down, Kendall got cold feet. Really cold feet. Okay, so the cool wood against her bare feet felt good compared to the heat rising up her neck into her face. She couldn't do this. She'd never been this forward in her entire life, always playing the good girl, refusing to give her brother any trouble after he'd taken on the huge responsibility of raising her when their parents had died in a car crash. Having just graduated high school, he'd barely been able to tie his own shoelaces and he'd never tied hers.

But Connor learned and attended the small college in town while showing up at all of her school events, shuttling her to and from soccer practice like any other soccer mom. He'd grown up before he'd had a chance to be a kid.

Kendall made life as easy on him as possible. She understood the sacrifice he'd made by giving up a scholarship to the University of Texas to stay home and care for his kid sister.

As soon as she graduated and was safely accepted to the local college, he'd gotten his commission into the U.S. Army and left Temptation, Texas. He'd only agreed to go on the condition his best friend would look out for his little sister.

Therein lay the problem. Some of the reasons for which Kendall had fallen in love with Ed were the same reasons he wouldn't look at her as other than Connor's little sister. He was loyal to his friends, protective to a fault, and he kept his word no matter what. And four years later, he was no different.

Connor had managed to miss being deployed for the first three of Kendall's college years, but now he was deployed and Kendall was about to graduate. If she was going to get Ed to notice her, it had to be soon.

She'd hoped when she turned twenty-one, Ed would start seeing her as a grown woman, not a kid sister. Two months had passed since her birthday and nothing had changed. After a come-to-Temptation meeting with her best friend, Lacey, she'd made the decision to take matters into her own hands and push the issue.

Thus Plan A of Operation Sex Ed. Let him see what he's missing.

Kendall still wasn't all that sure that standing practically naked in the window had done the trick. Ed had reacted just like Ed always reacted, all protective and big-brotherly.

Enter Plan B.

Kendall stood in front of Ed's door, her hand poised over the wood. "I can't do this."

From above, Lacey called out, "Yes. You. Can."

Kendall jumped and knocked on the door before she could change her mind. As she waited for Ed to answer, she realized she was still naked and carrying the tank top. Her heart palpitated as she shoved her arms through the shirt. She'd just pulled it down over her breasts when Ed jerked open the door.

He wore nothing but a towel wrapped around his middle, his hair and body dripping from his recent shower.

Desire slammed into her belly, spreading like wildfire, frying every brain cell to a crisp. For a moment, she couldn't remember why she'd come down the stairs, then Lacey's words echoed in her head. *Remember Plan B.* Smoothing the panic out of her face and voice, she smiled up at him. "Got a minute?" Without waiting for a response, she waltzed past him, inhaling the fresh scent of soap and Ed. As she sidled by, she swung her hips in such a manner as to invite just about any hot-blooded male to rutting season with a grown woman, not a little girl. She'd purposely not pulled her shirt over her rear, leaving her naked ass exposed to his view. The thong between her butt cheeks didn't count for anything.

"Got any clothes?" Ed asked, searching the hallway before he closed the door, turned and leaned on it. "Please tell me you don't run around like that in front of the kid that left as I was getting home?"

"Cory?" She faced Ed, twisting the hem of her tank top, drawing it up enough Ed could see the triangle of black lace that was the bulk of material in the thong panties. "He likes it when I dress like this." She stood straighter, her unbound breasts naturally jutting forward. "I didn't come to talk about Cory, I came to ask for your help."

"My help?" Ed glanced down at his towel. "Could it wait until I'm dressed?"

Kendall shrugged, her lips twisting in a teasing smile. "Dressed or undressed doesn't matter to me. I need lessons, and I can't think of anyone that I trust as much as I trust you to teach me."

"Exactly what kind of lessons did you have in mind?" Ed pushed away from the door and strode through the living room to the bedroom.

Kendall had to resist the urge to grab the towel and yank it loose. Her blood raced through her veins, molten hot for the man, and he wasn't aware she existed as anything other than Connor's sister. Why was fate so cruel?

She followed him, standing in the doorway of his bedroom, imagining lying naked in his bed, making mad passionate love. An ache built in her core, fortifying her determination to make Operation Sex Ed work.

Ed reached into his closet for a pair of jeans.

Kendall launched Plan B. "I need lessons on how to attract a man."

He spun to face her, dropping the jeans to the floor. His towel slipped and he barely caught it before it ended up with the jeans around his ankles. "What?"

Her gaze swept over his thick thighs and narrow hips, her pulse pounding in the vein at the base of her throat. "I want lessons on how to attract a man," she repeated more slowly, as if speaking to someone with limited faculties.

"I heard what you said, but what are you talking about?" He clutched his towel in front of him, the effect displaying a significant amount of leg, thigh, hips and groin.

Kendall licked her lips, her gaze fixed on the position still covered by the towel, willing Ed to expose even more. Her pussy creamed at the mere thought of seeing his cock. How would it be to hold it in her hands? Kendall's breath caught in her throat. In an attempt to concentrate, she pulled her glance up to his face. "I think I'm in love with a guy, but he doesn't have a clue I exist. I want you to help me attract his attention."

"Aren't you a little young for playing games with guys?"

"I'm not seventeen anymore, in case you hadn't noticed, and these," she pointed to her breasts, the nipples puckering on cue through the thin material of the tank top, "aren't getting any action. I need help."

Ed ran a hand through his hair, his gaze glancing off her breasts and hitting every corner of the room without looking back. "Tell me you didn't just say your...your...oh, hell, aren't getting any action."

"Boobs?" She raised her brows and stared at him. "I'm all grown up, Mr. Judson, not the little girl that used to follow you and Connor around."

"I know you're all grown up, but—"

"I'm twenty-one, single and almost finished with college." She jammed her hands onto her hips. "I deserve a sex-life just like anyone else. If you aren't going to help me figure this out, I'll find someone who will."

"Whoa, wait a minute."Ed held up his hands. "Just exactly what is it you want me to teach you? Not that I'm agreeing to this lunacy."

"I want you to show me what turns on a guy. Kind of like a sex education class for dummies. Only I'm not planning on practicing the abstinence part." Her hands skimmed over her breasts, curving down over her hips. "I want the full-blown, how-to-make-him-hot-for-me lessons."

"Holy Hell, you're kidding, right?"

"Do I look like I'm kidding?" She tapped a bare foot, realizing it probably wasn't making a big impression with her bright pink toenail polish. "Not only am I not kidding, I want lessons to begin tonight. And in payment for lessons, the pizza is on me."

"Pizza?"

The knock on the door couldn't have been timed better.

"Right on time." She smiled and fished the twenty-dollar bill out of the triangle of her panties. "I'll be right back. Don't go anywhere, we have work to do."

"Pizza?" Ed stood for a moment as though rooted to the floor, his hand still clutching the towel around his middle, his face pale, probably in shock.

Good. Kendall turned toward the door and called out, "Coming!"

She hadn't taken two steps when Ed caught up

with her, ripped the twenty from her fingers and shoved her back in the bedroom. "Stay," he commanded.

Then, wearing nothing but the towel and carrying the twenty, he opened the door to the apartment for Jason, the pizza delivery boy.

"Nice towel." Jason shoved the pizza box at Ed.

For a moment, Ed fumbled with the towel, the twenty and the pizza box.

Kendall fought back the urge to giggle, silently praying he'd slip and drop the towel.

Sadly, Ed managed to pay for the pizza and close the door behind Jason, towel intact around his middle.

Kendall came out into the living room, crossed her arms beneath her chest, giving them a little added lift. "So what's it to be? Will you teach me everything you know about making love, or do I take my pizza elsewhere?"

ABOUT THE AUTHOR

Twenty years of livin' and lovin' on a South Texas ranch raising horses, cattle, goats, ostriches and emus left an indelible impression on Myla Jackson, one she likes to instill in her red-hot stories. Myla pens wildly sexy, fun adventures of all genres including historical westerns, medieval tales, romantic suspense, contemporary romance and paranormal beasties of all shapes and sexy sizes. She lives in the tree-covered hills of Northwest Arkansas with her husband of more than 20 years and her muses—the human-wanna-be canines—Chewy and Sweetpea.

To learn more about Myla Jackson and her alter ego Elle James
visit:
www.mylajackson.com
mylajackson@mylajackson.com